She'd Found Herself a Killer...

If a woman wanted a man to do something violent for her, she couldn't pick a better place than the Barbary Coast, where the bars catered to the dregs of humanity, drunkards, braggarts, cutthroats—and killers.

Clint followed her to a small saloon on a side street. A man stepped from the doorway and rushed forward to embrace her. Then he stiffened and staggered back.

The knife was sticking out from his belly, and he was staring at her in horror...

Also in THE GUNSMITH series

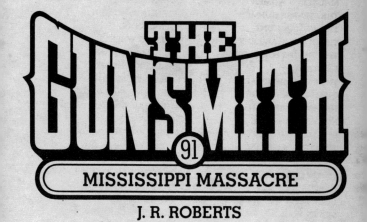

THE GUNSMITH

91

MISSISSIPPI MASSACRE

J. R. ROBERTS

JOVE BOOKS, NEW YORK

THE GUNSMITH #91: MISSISSIPPI MASSACRE

A Jove book/published by arrangement with
the author

PRINTING HISTORY
Jove edition/July 1989

ISBN: 0-515-10063-3

Jove books are published by The Berkley Publishing Group,
200 Madison Avenue, New York, New York 10016.
The name "JOVE" and the "J" logo
are trademarks belonging to Jove Publications, Inc.

PRINTED IN THE UNITED STATES OF AMERICA

10 9 8 7 6 5 4 3 2 1

MISSISSIPPI MASSACRE

PROLOGUE

Clint Adams had four days to keep Justin Tarr from being hanged.

Justin was supposed to have killed a young woman when he attempted to rape her and she resisted. Clint knew that Justin would never try to rape a woman. In fact, he rarely had difficulty attracting women, so he wouldn't *have* to rape one. If anything, women were constantly after *him*.

Tarr's story was that he had never met this young woman, and yet the New Orleans Police had come to his hotel and arrested him. He was tried and by the testimony of an "eyewitness" was convicted.

It wasn't until after he was convicted that he sent word to his friend, Clint Adams, that he was in trouble.

"Why the hell did you wait until you were convicted to call for my help, Justin?" Clint Adams asked through the bars of Justin Tarr's cell.

1

Justin was a handsome man in his early thirties. He stared at Clint with eyes some women had described as "soulful." Right now all Clint Adams saw in those eyes was "fear."

Justin shook his head as if trying to dispel a fog and said, "I'm innocent, Clint. It never occurred to me that they would actually *convict* me."

"Justin, Justin," Clint said, shaking his head now. "I'd forgotten how naive you are."

"Clint," Justin said, gripping the bars tightly, "I need your help."

"Just like the last time," Clint said.

"Yes," Justin Tarr said, "just like the last time."

ONE

San Francisco, 15 months ago

The first time Clint Adams saw Justin Tarr was in a Portsmouth Square hotel called the Alhambra, in the casino. He was standing at the faro table with a woman on each arm. The women were actually what Clint had noticed first.

The woman on Tarr's right arm was a tall, willowy brunette with naturally dark skin. She did not have an ounce of fat on her. The woman on the left arm was a busty blonde. She was some years older than the brunette, but she wore the extra mileage very well. She was full-bodied and, by all appearances, quite bored.

It was the blonde who actually *held* Clint's attention after that initial moment. He studied her appreciatively and then turned his attention to the man she and the brunette were with.

Justin Tarr.

Tarr was a tall man. He had dark, curly hair, a firm,

3

cleft jaw, broad shoulders but delicate hands. His hands looked as if they had never done a hard day's work in their life—unless it was with a deck of cards.

The man was obviously a gambler.

Clint didn't like faro, but he approached the table and watched the man and the two women. The man was playing, urged on by the brunette, who obviously appreciated every move the man made. The blonde still seemed bored with the proceedings.

The man was winning steadily, to the delight of the brunette. The blonde still seemed a bit distracted and was now looking around the room. She still had not relinquished her hold on the man's left arm, though— until she saw Clint Adams.

Their eyes met and, very slowly, she slid her hand off the man's arm. Clint was about to approach her when another man moved up to them and grabbed Tarr —whose name Clint still did not know—by the shoulder, spun him around and hit him on that fine, firm jaw.

Tarr fell against the faro table, almost upsetting it, and then slid to the floor, his hands crossed in front of his face to ward off any following blow. The man who had hit him drew back a foot to kick the fallen man, and that was when Clint moved.

He caught the man's foot from behind and pulled on it. The man immediately lost his balance and went crashing to the floor. Clint quickly moved out of the man's way as he fell.

"Up we go," Clint said, helping Tarr up.

Tarr looked beyond Clint at the man on the floor and then said to him, "Thank you. I am not a physical man. He might have kicked my face in."

Clint looked at Tarr and said, "Well, we couldn't

have that, could we?" and then he looked at the blonde.

"No," she said, holding his eyes with her own, "we certainly couldn't."

Clint's warning was a loud gasp from the brunette. He turned and saw that the other man had risen and was coming toward him.

"Back off," Clint said, warningly.

"Jack, no!" the brunette cried out.

"Bitch!" the man said, and that was when Clint realized that he was after the brunette, and not him.

"Jack—" she said, again, this time in a different tone of voice.

"Hey," Clint said, moving smoothly between her and the man.

"Get out of my way!"

"Calm down, friend," Clint said. "Let's talk about it."

"Talk, hell," the man said. "That bitch is my wife!"

Clint turned and looked at the brunette for confirmation or denial. Tarr was also looking at her, with more interest than before. Apparently the possibility that she might be another man's wife made her that much more attractive to him.

It was roughly the same punch that the man had used on Tarr, but where Tarr had fallen Clint merely staggered back a step or two. He righted himself immediately and caught the man's next punch on his forearm. Instead of hitting him back he stiff-armed him, striking the man's chest with the heel of his hand.

"Ease up!" he said. "I didn't come here for a fight."

"Is there some problem here?" a man asked, approaching them. Obviously, he worked for the hotel.

Clint turned to the brunette and asked, "Is this man your husband?"

"He used to be," she said, "but not anymore."

"Is this man bothering you?" the hotel employee asked.

"Yes," Justin Tarr said.

"No," Clint said.

The hotel man looked confused and looked to the blonde for help.

"Hell," she said, looking amused, "he's not bothering me."

The brunette touched Tarr's arm and said, "I'll be right back." She moved to her former husband's side—if indeed he *was* her former husband—took his arm and said, "Come outside, Jack."

"Heather—"

"Let's talk outside," she said, soothingly. She looked at the hotel man and said, "There's no problem, here."

The hotel man looked around at everyone involved, and at the crowd which had gathered to watch, and said, "All right, but no more disturbances."

"Sure," Clint said.

The brunette walked off with "Jack" in tow and the hotel man walked away. The crowd went back to what they were doing before the entertainment had begun.

Clint looked at the blonde and said, "Clint Adams."

He was surprised when she stuck out her hand and said, "Marcy Truman." He took her hand and found her grip remarkably firm.

"My name is Justin Tarr," Tarr said to Clint.

Clint reluctantly pulled his eyes from the blonde's and looked at Tarr.

"You should be more careful who you associate with, Mr. Tarr."

"I didn't know she was married."

"Would it have mattered if you had?" Marcy Truman asked him.

With an ingenuous look on his face Tarr said, "No." Then he frowned and asked Marcy, "Are you married?"

"Would it matter if I was?"

"No."

"What about you?" she said, turning to Clint.

"What about me . . . what?"

"Would it matter to you if I was married?"

Clint looked at her and said, "That would depend on what we were planning to do."

"Well," she said, regarding him with real interest, "there are several possibilities. . . . And no, I'm not married."

Moments later the brunette reappeared, took hold of Justin Tarr's right arm again and said, "It's all right, now."

The blonde hesitated a moment as Justin Tarr turned his attention back to the faro table, and then took hold of Clint's arm.

TWO

Clint spent the rest of the evening with Justin Tarr, Marcy and the brunette, Heather. They had dinner, did some gambling, and then Justin asked Heather to go to his room with him.

She agreed, readily.

That left Clint with Marcy, and they went to the hotel dining room for a nightcap.

"What do you think of him?" she asked.

"Tarr?"

"Yes."

Clint thought a moment, then shook his head helplessly.

"I like him," he said, "and I don't know why."

"He's different," she said. "I've never met anyone like him, before."

"I haven't, either."

"I don't like him," Marcy said.

"Why were you with him tonight, then?"

She shrugged and said, "I had nothing else to do, and how was I to know I wouldn't like him?"

"And me?"

"And you . . . what?"

"Do you like me?"

She leaned forward, touched his hand, and said, "You I liked right away."

Her breasts were very full and firm, but they still dangled in his face as she rode him. His rigid cock was buried inside of her and as she bounced up and down on him he tried to capture the nipples in his mouth. Finally he became frustrated. He put his arms around her back and pulled her down so that he could suck them. She continued to rotate her hips, moaning as the dual sensations caused by his penis and his mouth brought her closer and closer to the moment of climax.

And then she was there . . .

Clint was staying in a hotel just off Portsmouth Square, and that's where they had gone to make love.

Marcy was energetic, inventive and totally free of inhibitions in bed. It was one of the most satisfying nights of sex he'd ever experienced.

She was so good she seemed almost . . . professional.

"What's wrong, Clint?" she asked, later.

"You're very good," he said, after a pause.

"So are you."

"No," he said, "I mean you're *very* good."

She turned her head on the pillow so that she was looking at him. Her hair was matted to her head by perspiration.

"Oh," she said, "I see. You want to know if I do this for a living."

"Actually," he said, "I *don't* want to know. What you should know is that I don't pay for sex."

"All right."

"What do you mean, 'all right'?" he asked.

"I mean all right, you don't pay for sex. Did I say I expected to be paid?"

"Well . . . no."

After a moment he asked, "Does that mean you do or you don't?"

"Do or don't what?"

"Do this for a living?"

"I thought you said you didn't want to know."

He regarded her for a moment, then turned his whole body to face her and said, "Never let it be said that I wasn't a man of my word."

He pulled her to him and kissed her. They were both still damp from their first session of lovemaking. Her flesh stuck to his as they kissed, and when he moved away from her it was almost as if they peeled apart.

He bent his head to her firm breasts and sucked first one nipple, and then the other. She moaned and cupped his head in her hands. Exerting pressure, she guided his head down further, over her belly, until his face was nestled between her legs. His tongue delved into her and then moved over her in long, languid strokes as he enjoyed the taste of her.

"Oooh, yes Clint, yes, that's it, right there, that's the place . . ." she said, encouraging him. When his tongue centered on her clit her hips jumped and she released his head and gathered the sheet into her hands, twisting it as he continued to suck her.

"Oh, God!" she moaned, as his tongue began to lash

out at her, flicking over her, bringing her closer and closer to climax, again.

"Up," she pleaded, groping for him, "up, please, I need you in me . . ."

He mounted her then and thrust into her, and she exploded beneath him, writhing as if she were trying to get out from under him, and at the same time closer to him . . .

He watched her dress.

"You didn't ask me to stay the night," she said when she finished. There was no hint of reproach in her tone. It was just a statement.

"Then I wouldn't have gotten to watch you dress."

"You could have watched in the morning."

"In the morning I would have left before you."

She smiled and said, "I almost believe you."

She leaned over the bed and kissed him, a lingering yet somewhat chaste kiss.

As she started for the door he said, "Hey?"

"What?"

"Why weren't you expecting me to pay you?"

"I could say that I'm not a pro," she said, "but the truth of the matter is that Justin paid in advance."

"And Heather?"

"What about her?"

"Was she paid in advance?"

She shrugged. "As far as I know, she's not a pro."

"Wait a minute," he said, frowning, sitting up in bed. "He paid you, and not her, and he went to bed with her?"

"I suppose so."

"Why?"

"Maybe he liked her better."

"Impossible!"

She smiled at that and said, "Some men like younger women."

"It's a foolish man who chooses youth over experience," he said.

She smiled again and said, "I knew I liked you for some reason."

"My body?"

She shook her head.

"Your mind."

She left then and he laid back down, thinking first about her and then about Justin Tarr.

He was curious enough about the man to want to get to know more about him, to try and find out why he liked a man who could so easily have been disliked.

THREE

Clint went back to the Alhambra Hotel, where Justin Tarr was staying. He found out from the desk clerk what room Justin was in and went upstairs. When he knocked on the door, it was answered by the brunette from the night before, Heather. She was wearing a man's shirt that covered just enough and left her long legs bare. Clint thought that she had legs like the stems of long-stemmed roses.

"Heather what?" he asked.

"What?"

"Heather . . . ?"

"Oh," she said, blinking rapidly, "O'Day, Heather O'Day."

"Is Tarr in?"

"He's here."

"Can I talk to him?"

"Sure," she said. "He's having breakfast, but come on in."

She stepped back and Clint moved past her into the room. She closed the door behind them.

Tarr was seated at a serving table on wheels, eating breakfast. There was a second plate, which indicated that Heather had been eating as well.

"Clint," Justin Tarr said, as Heather sat across from him and began to eat.

"I'm sorry to interrupt your breakfast, Justin."

"Nonsense," Justin said. "Pull over another chair and we'll share with you."

"I don't want anything to eat, thanks."

"Fine," Justin said, "then have a cup of coffee."

"Thanks," Clint said, "that offer I'll take you up on."

"Take what you want," Justin said. "What's mine is yours. After last night I owe you."

"You don't owe me anything."

Clint poured himself a cup of coffee and sipped it. Heather ate in silence, occasionally looking up at Justin.

"What brings you around this morning, Clint, if it's not to collect on a debt?" Justin asked.

"I'm curious."

"Oh? About what?"

"About you."

"What about me? Ask away. My life's an open book."

"I'm curious about who you are," Clint said, "what you're doing in San Francisco. I'd like to know why you hire a whore, pay her in advance, and then let her go with me?"

"Why not?" Justin said, shrugging. "You helped me last night when I needed it, when a lot of other people would have stood by and watched me get my face kicked in. You're my friend, aren't you?"

Clint hesitated and then said, "Let's just say acquaintance, for now."

"You call it acquaintance," Justin said. "To me you're a new friend. How was she, by the way?"

Clint didn't answer.

"Clint is a gentleman, Justin," Heather said. "He won't answer that kind of question."

"Why not?" Justin asked. He seemed genuinely puzzled by her remark.

"Because he's a gentleman."

Again, Justin seemed puzzled.

"Tell him how I was in bed, Justin," Heather said.

Justin looked at Clint and said, "She was fine."

"Just fine?" Heather asked.

"You were wonderful," Justin said to her.

"Where are you from, Justin?" Clint asked, to change the subject.

"The East," Justin said. "I was born in St. Louis, Missouri. My father is a banker there, and a very rich man. I got bored with living there and came west."

"Looking for what?"

Justin shrugged. "Excitement."

"And have you found it?"

"From time to time, yes," Justin said, "but I have to keep moving around, constantly looking for more."

"And what do you do for money?"

Justin looked at Clint as if he were crazy and said, "When I run low, my father sends me some." It was as if that was the only possible answer.

"So your only responsibility is to have fun and find excitement?"

Justin shrugged and said, "Sure."

"No worries, huh?"

"Only something like last night," Justin said. "You know, when somebody wants to get violent. I'm not very good at that."

"And what would have happened if I hadn't been around to help you?"

Justin shrugged. "Something else would have happened, I guess," he said. "I'm lucky that way."

"You can't depend on luck and your father for the rest of your life," Clint said.

"I've done all right, so far," Justin said, "haven't I, Heather?"

"You're doing just fine, Justin," Heather said, because it was what he wanted to hear.

Clint looked at the two of them and could only shake his head.

"You've got a lot to learn, Justin," he said.

"About what?"

"About the real world."

"The real world isn't so wonderful," Heather said, and Clint could hear the bitterness in her voice.

"That depends on you," Clint said. "Just because you had a bad marriage, Heather—"

"I had a terrible marriage," Heather said, correcting him. "Not a bad marriage, a terrible—a *disastrous* marriage!"

"What was so bad about it?"

Heather gave Clint a hard stare now, and her face became harder and less attractive. The skin over her cheeks seemed to be pulled extra tight now, and he thought he could see the shape of her skull.

"How can you ask me that?" she demanded. "You saw Jack last night. You saw what he's like."

"I saw a jealous man who still loves you."

"You saw a violent man who still wants to possess me, like I was a piece of . . . of property!"

"What is Justin, Heather?"

Justin looked up from his breakfast, interested in the answer to that himself.

"Justin . . . Justin is gentle, and interesting . . . and . . . and . . ."

"And he's rich, isn't he?"

"So?" she said. "He's rich. What's wrong with that?"

"Nothing," Clint said, putting down his empty coffee cup. "There's nothing wrong with it. You go right ahead and enjoy Justin's money."

Clint looked at Justin.

"It's not my money," Justin said, "it's my father's money."

"That's the first really honest statement I've heard you make since I met you."

"Honest?" Justin repeated, frowning.

"Do you know what the word means, Justin?"

"Well . . . sure, sure I do."

"Do you, Heather?"

"Of course I do."

"But I'll bet neither one of you ever think about it," Clint said, "do you?"

"Not much," Justin admitted, readily.

"Not a lot," Heather admitted, and turned her attention to her food again.

Clint shook his head again, deciding that he didn't really like these two people much, after all.

"You two are made for each other," he said, and started for the door.

He had almost reached it when there was a knock on it. He turned and looked toward Justin.

"Would you get that for me?" Justin asked.

"Sure," Clint said. "I'm on my way out, anyway."

He opened the door and saw two men standing there. One was a uniformed policeman. The other man was dressed in a suit, but Clint assumed that he was a policeman, as well—probably the other man's superior. He was older than the uniformed man, and his eyes looked as if they had seen a lot more.

"Are you Justin Tarr?" the man in the suit asked.

"No, I'm not."

The man frowned and asked, "Is this Justin Tarr's room?"

"It is."

"Is he here?"

"He is."

Exasperated the man said, "Can I see him?"

"What's going on, Clint?" Justin asked, coming up behind him.

"Are you Justin Tarr?" the man asked.

"Yes, I am."

"Mr. Tarr," the policeman said, "it is my duty to inform you that you are under arrest for murder. Come with me, please."

FOUR

"Hold on a moment," Clint said. "What's he under arrest for?"

The man looked at Clint and asked, "Who are you, sir?"

"My name is Clint Adams," he said, and before he could add anything else Justin jumped in and said, "He's my friend."

"Well, *friend*," the man said, "your friend is under arrest for murder, and I suggest you stay out of the way."

"By the way," Clint said, "who are you?"

The man looked annoyed at being caught out and said, "My name is Inspector Deal of the San Francisco Police Department."

"Well, Inspector Deal," Clint said, "don't you think Mr. Tarr deserves to know who he was supposed to have killed?"

"Yeah," Justin said, "who?"

"Do you know a man named Crawford?" Deal asked Justin.

"Crawford?" Justin repeated. "No, I don't."

"Jack Crawford?"

"I don't know any Crawford, Jack or otherwise," Justin said.

"Mr. Tarr—"

"Inspector—" Clint said.

"Please don't interfere, Mr. . . . ."

"Adams."

"Mr. Adams," Deal said. "Don't interfere. Come along, Mr. Tarr."

"But I never met a man named Crawford!" Justin said, real fear beginning to show in his eyes.

"Mr. Tarr, I could have Officer Nettles here help you to come along, if you like . . ."

"That won't be necessary, Inspector," Clint said.

"But Clint—"

"Go with them, Justin."

"Clint—"

"Go with them."

Deal looked at Clint and said, "Thank you, Mr. Adams. That's very good advice."

Justin wasn't fully dressed so he went inside to put on his shirt and jacket and came back to the door.

"Let me get this straight, all right?" Justin asked.

"Yes?" Deal said, losing his patience.

"You are arresting me for killing a man named Jack Crawford?"

"For *suspicion* of having killed him, yes."

"But . . . I don't know the man."

"We'll sort this all out at the station, Mr. Tarr," Deal said. "Now come along . . . *please*."

"Clint," Justin said, imploring Clint with his eyes, "you'll come with me, won't you?"

"You need a lawyer, Mr. Tarr," Inspector Deal said, "not a friend."

"I don't know any lawyers."

"I'll find you a lawyer, Justin," Clint said. "Meanwhile, just cooperate."

"Good advice, Mr. Tarr," Deal said. "It will go much easier for you if you cooperate."

"All right," Tarr said, "all right."

They started down the hall and Clint called out, "Inspector."

"Yes?"

"I'll be coming to the station with a lawyer," Clint said. "If I find Mr. Tarr in anything but perfect health—"

"Don't threaten me, Mr. Adams," Deal said. "Not in my own town."

"Just remember . . ." Clint said.

FIVE

There were some other things that didn't surprise Clint Adams that time in San Francisco.

One was that Justin Tarr did *not* kill Jack Crawford.

The other thing was that Heather O'Day Crawford did.

Oh, she didn't do it herself. She had a lover do it, but she and the lover both figured that Justin Tarr would be the perfect patsy. And they were right, except for one thing.

Clint Adams.

Heather's reaction to the arrest of Justin Tarr bothered Clint, so instead of going for a lawyer right away, he took up a position across from the Alhambra, and waited for Heather Crawford to come out.

He hadn't long to wait.

Heather came out ten minutes later, walking very

quickly. Without a glance behind her she started away from the Alhambra, and Clint followed her.

When Heather spoke about her husband there seemed to be a lot of bitterness—possibly enough to even foster hatred.

Was there enough hatred there to lead to murder? That was the question.

Clint followed Heather out of Portsmouth Square and for a while he had no idea where Heather was going, but soon it became apparent.

She was going to the Barbary Coast.

Now, if a woman wanted a man who would do something violent for her, she couldn't pick a better place than the Barbary Coast. As highbrow as Portsmouth Square was, that's how lowbrow the coast was. The bars there catered to the dregs of humanity, the drunkards, the braggarts, the shanghaiers, the robbers, the cutthroats, and its fair share of killers.

It was Clint Adams's bet that Heather O'Day Crawford had found herself a killer.

Clint knew that Justin would be waiting nervously in his cell—hopefully in good health—for him to appear with a lawyer, but it seemed to Clint that it would serve Justin even better if he could arrive with the killer—or killers—in tow.

Following Heather down the streets of the Barbary Coast was a lot easier than following her through the other areas of San Francisco. For one thing most of the men she past were looking her over, some of them making rude remarks to her. She was walking very fast and didn't dare look back for fear of encouraging one or more of them. As far as Clint was concerned, the men ignored him. (Of course, some of the street whores approached him, but he brushed them off wordlessly.)

He followed her through some of the worst streets of the coast until she finally came to her destination. It was a small saloon on a side street, only she didn't go in the front way. She went around to the side alley and knocked on a door there. Clint watched from a doorway as the door opened, bathing her in yellow light. A man stepped from the doorway and they embraced passionately before they entered the room together.

It was looking better and better, Clint thought, as he slid into the darkened alley.

There was one window in the alley, and as he peered into it a light flared from inside. He pulled back and watched from the corner of the window as Heather and the man entered what appeared to be an office. Clint assumed that the man owned the saloon, and this then was the office behind the place. The other door in the room would probably lead to the saloon itself.

Clint watched as first they embraced again, and then Heather stepped back and said something. As hard as Clint strained he couldn't hear what was being said, but the mere fact that Heather had rushed here from the Alhambra could not be just coincidence.

Clint studied the man. He was a big man, coarse looking, in his thirties, and he realized why the man looked familiar.

He reminded Clint of Jack Crawford.

Apparently, the same type of man fell for Heather, and she was using that to her advantage. Clint felt more and more strongly that Heather and this man had been the ones to do poor Jack in. He wondered what she had in store for this man, now that he had upheld his part of the bargain.

Surely not what she had promised.

His question was answered only moments after it had

occurred to him. She held one arm out for the man, who rushed to embrace her, and then he stiffened and staggered back. The knife that she obviously had concealed in her other hand was sticking out from his belly, and he was staring at her in horror.

Clint rushed to the side door and, as luck would have it, it was not locked.

He slipped into a hallway and quickly turned left and approached the room Heather and the man were in.

". . . didn't really think I had you kill my husband so I could go away with you, did you, Mark?" she was saying.

Jesus, that was as good as a confession!

"B—b—but—" the wounded man stammered, and then Clint heard something that led him to believe the man had fallen to the floor.

"Now I'm rid of him, *and* you," Heather said.

Clint stepped into the room and saw her standing over the man. He was lying on his back, his hands around the knife, and his eyes were still open.

He was still alive.

"That was pretty slick, Heather," he said from behind her.

She turned quickly and stared at him.

"You!" she said. Suddenly, her face changed and she said, "Oh, I'm so glad you're here, Clint." She rushed to him, but he backed away.

"Not so fast, Heather. You might have another knife hidden in your skirts somewhere."

"Clint . . . he—he attacked me. He said he killed Jack so we could be together. I never suspected—"

"Forget it, Heather," Clint said. "I'm not as gullible as some men, where you're concerned."

"But Clint—"

There was a chair in the corner of the room. Clint pulled Heather to him and she opened her mouth, mistaking his intention. He turned her around and pushed her towards the chair. She backpedaled, hit the chair and sat down hard in it.

"Stay right there," he told her.

"Clint—" she said, starting to rise. He saw her eyes dart to the hall door.

"Heather, if you try and leave I'll have to shoot you."

She stared at him, decided that he meant it and sat back down.

Clint went to the other door, opened it and saw that it did indeed open into the saloon. There was a table right near the door with two men sitting at it.

"Hey, you two?"

They looked up and one of them said, "Us?"

"Yes, you. Come here for a moment."

"What for?" the other asked.

They both looked like seamen who were looking for a ship.

"For five dollars each."

They sprang to their feet, one of them knocking over his chair, and hurried over to the door.

"Inside," Clint said, and they slid past him.

When they saw the man on the floor one of them said, "Holy Jesus!"

"That's Mark Colby," the other said. "What happened to him?"

"Ask him," Clint said. "He's still alive."

The man who had identified Colby went to the fallen man, knelt by him and said, "Who did this, Mark. This fella?"

Colby, sweating heavily and pale as a ghost, shook

his head and stammered, "W—weren't . . . him. It . . . it was . . . was . . . her!"

Both men looked at Heather, who was sitting with her hands folded in her lap.

"The woman stabbed you?" the second man asked.

Colby nodded his head and Clint saw his eyes start to glaze over.

"Y—yes," he said, "I ki—killed her hu—husband for her . . . and sh—she's . . . killed me."

And with that Mark Colby died.

Clint looked at Heather, who looked crestfallen, and said, "That's two witnesses, Heather. I think we'd better go and see the police."

"What about our five dollars?" the man by the door asked.

"Come with me and talk to the police, and I'll make it ten," Clint said.

"The police?" the man by the door said, rubbing his hand over his face.

The first man was not quite as money hungry, nor was he as afraid of the police. "This woman's killed Mark, Harry. We got to talk to the police." He looked at Clint and said, "I'll go with you, mister."

"A—all right," the other man said, "so will I."

Clint stared at the two men. Heather had come to the Barbary Coast looking for a man who would kill for her, and now two men were going to do the right thing and testify against her.

You found all kinds on the Barbary Coast, Clint thought.

Fifteen months later Clint was staring at Justin Tarr through bars, and the man had the same desperate look he'd had in San Francisco, when he'd been arrested.

"Justin," Clint said, "you should have learned from San Francisco."

"I swear, Clint," Justin said, "I never even met the woman."

"Well, whose toes have you stepped on, this time?"

"Nobody's!"

"Have you been winning?"

"Sure," Justin said, "I usually win."

"Then you must have stepped on somebody's toes," Clint said, standing up.

"Where are you going?"

Clint looked at him and said, "To start looking at people's feet for smashed toes. Don't go away."

"Where am I going to go?"

Clint started out of the cell area, then turned back and said, "I suppose you don't want your father notified this time, either?"

In San Francisco Justin had refused to wire his father in St. Louis about the situation.

"Are you kidding?" he said. "I'd never get another cent."

"And you'd have to go back to banking."

"I'd almost rather be dead than do that, Clint."

"All right, Justin," Clint said, "I'll see what I can do, this time."

"Clint!" Justin called as Clint started away.

"What?"

"Almost," Justin said. "I said I'd *almost* rather be dead."

Clint nodded, waved and said, "I heard you, Justin."

SIX

After Clint left Justin Tarr he was shown back to the office of the chief of police of New Orleans, Daniel Thoreau.

Upon arrival at the New Orleans Police Station Clint had asked for Inspector DuBois. It had saddened him to discover that the inspector—who he had met several years ago—had been killed shortly thereafter.

Aside from a sense of personal loss, this left Clint with no contact within the police department.

"I've poured some brandy," Chief Thoreau informed him as he entered.

"Thank you, Chief."

"What did your, er, friend tell you?"

Clint sat opposite the chief and said, "That he was innocent."

"And, of course, you believe him."

"I do."

"Of course."

"I'd like to be able to talk to the police officer who arrested him."

"That would be Inspector Chevalier. I won't stop him from talking to you, but neither will I order him to. It will be up to him."

"Would there be any reason why he wouldn't want to talk to me?" Clint asked, curiously.

The police chief shrugged.

"I cannot speak for Emil—er, Inspector Chevalier."

"Where will I find him?"

"On duty here, tomorrow morning," the chief said.

"He's not here tonight?"

"Alas, no, he has gone off duty."

"And you wouldn't tell me where he lives, would you?"

"Of course not."

"I didn't think so." Clint sipped the brandy, found it excellent and said so.

"Thank you."

It would take more than complimenting the man's brandy to get him to cooperate. Clint finished the brandy and stood up.

"Did my friend have any property that was taken from him?"

"He did."

"May I have it?"

"I will have to clear that with him."

"He'll allow it."

"Nevertheless, I will have to ask him."

"And when can you do that?"

"Tomorrow. If he agrees, you may pick the property up in the morning."

"Thank you, Chief."

"Your friend is guilty, Mr. Adams. I don't think you should waste your time trying to prove otherwise."

Clint stopped and stared at the man, searching for some sort of implied threat.

"Is there some other reason why I shouldn't pursue this?"

"No," the chief said, "except . . ."

"Except what?"

"Well, the girl he killed was a member of a rather prominent family here in New Orleans."

"I see," Clint said. "A prominent and powerful family, no doubt."

"Exactly."

"And you can't be responsible for what they might do to someone who was trying to help my friend."

The man shrugged. "Naturally, if they broke the law I would be forced to enforce it, but I would prefer that the situation didn't arise."

"That could only be avoided if I left town."

"Yes, indeed."

"Which I don't intend to do."

The man gave him a pitying smile. "I didn't expect that you would."

"One more thing, Chief."

"Yes?"

"What hotel was my friend staying in?"

"The Napoleon."

Clint was staying at the New Orleans House. He would have to switch over to the Napoleon tonight. Maybe he could even get the same room.

"Chief, I thank you for your help."

The man raised his hands helplessly.

"As I said, I believe you will be wasting your time, but I understand one's loyalty to one's friend."

Clint was tempted to make fun of the man by saying, "One is grateful that you do," but he decided against it. There was no need to antagonize him.

"I will see you in the morning, then," Clint said.

"Please," the chief said, "try to enjoy your stay in New Orleans."

"I'll do my best," Clint said, and left.

His hotel was walking distance from the police station and he was deep in thought as he covered the distance. Later he chided himself for being so deep in thought that he could be caught unawares. As it was, it was only his uncanny instinct for survival that kept him from being seriously injured.

He hadn't noticed the man falling in behind him, but his instincts had alerted him to the man approaching him. The walk was too narrow for both of them, and Clint, noticing that the other man was larger than he was, stepped off of it to give the man room.

"Hey," the man said, stepping into his path and putting a huge hand against his chest, "you think I'm so fat you got to step off the walk to let me by?"

Clint didn't know if the man was drunk or just looking for a fight, but he didn't want any part of him in either case.

"I was just trying to be friendly," Clint said.

"Friendly? You call telling me I'm fat being friendly?" the man asked.

"I didn't say you were fat," Clint said. He realized now that the man wasn't drunk. He was obviously looking for a fight.

"I got to teach you a lesson, stranger," the man said.

"No . . ." Clint started to say, and that was when instinct cut in. He "felt" something happening behind him and sidestepped as quickly as he could. If he was wrong he would just look foolish. That was better than having your head opened up.

"Look out!" the big man said, but he wasn't talking to Clint, he was talking to the man who'd been about to hit Clint on the head with a stout piece of wood. Clint, by stepping aside, threw the smaller man off balance. The piece of wood descended and struck the big man on the wrist. The sound of cracking bone was so audible that Clint winced.

"Jesus, Moses!" the big man shouted, grabbing his wounded wrist. "Ethan, by God—"

The smaller man, Ethan, turned and looked at Clint in shock.

"I was trying—" Ethan began, but Clint stepped in and hit him in the face. Ethan howled and fell over backwards, both hands going to his face. There was blood on Clint's hand, so he knew that the man's nose was bleeding.

"You fellas need to rehearse this a little better," he said, and turned and headed for his hotel, still aware of the alternating cries of pain from behind him.

An attempted robbery, he thought.

Later, he'd realized how wrong he was.

SEVEN

Ethan Colbert's nose was swollen.

John Colbert's right wrist was broken.

Robert Colbert—pronounced *Col-bear*—was upset.

"The man threw one punch?" he asked in disbelief.

"Yes, sir," Ethan said.

"Then how did you both get injured?"

"Uh—" John Colbert said.

"I, uh, broke John's wrist."

"What?" Robert Colbert said. "What?"

"I broke—"

"I heard you!"

Ethan, at twenty-nine, was four years older than his brother, who was arguably the strongest man in New Orleans. John seemed intent on proving that in countless barroom brawls.

Robert, at fifty-one, was the Colbert patriarch, and

expected more from his sons than they were ever able to give him.

His one joy in life had been Ana, his twenty-two-year-old daughter, and now she was dead, murdered by that . . . that fast talking gambler!

And now this man, Adams—according to his hotel register—was here to try and help the gambler, Tarr, get off.

Well, Robert Colbert wasn't going to have it.

"You were suppose to frighten him," he said to his sons, "warn him out of town."

"We tried, Poppa," Ethan said.

"Don't call me that!" Colbert snapped. "Your sister used to call me that."

"Yes, Pop—yes, sir."

In the corner of the plush living room was Alicia Colbert. At forty-eight she was still a vibrant, lovely woman. Right now her lovely face was drawn, marked by concern and even a little anger.

"All right," Colbert said, "go and get some rest. Did you both see a doctor?"

"Yes, sir," Ethan said.

"Go to bed, then."

"I'm sorry, Pop—uh, I'm sorry—" John stammered.

"Go to bed, John!" Colbert snapped.

"Yes, sir."

Both boys—men to be sure, but to their father still boys—left the room and went upstairs to their bedrooms.

With their sons gone Alicia Colbert turned her anger on her husband.

"You sent them out to beat a man up?" she demanded. "A stranger?"

"He's here to help that . . . gambler."

"How do you know that?"

"I know."

"Oh, of course," she said. "The great Robert Colbert. You own New Orleans, right? You know everything that goes on in New Orleans, right? Did you know that your daughter was going to be murdered, like a whore—"

"Quiet!" Colbert shouted. "Quiet, damn you!"

"I'll be quiet," Alicia said, not fazed by her husband's outburst. "I'll be so quiet you won't even know I'm here—and maybe I won't be!"

With that she turned and stalked from the room, leaving Robert Colbert alone with his grief.

He was sure that he was the only one who mourned the death of his sweet Ana. John was too stupid, Ethan too self-interested, and Alicia—well, Ana was as beautiful as Alicia had once been, and Robert had always felt that there was a certain amount of jealousy there. Alicia was still beautiful, but Ana's beauty had been so stunning . . . so breathtaking . . . men would flock to her . . . men like that . . . that gambler!

Justin Tarr was going to pay for killing his baby. One way or another—legally or not—he was going to pay!

Upstairs Alicia Colbert examined herself in her full length mirror. She was still beautiful, she thought, as she dropped her gown to the floor to stand naked. Her breasts were remarkably firm for a woman her age, as were her buttocks and her legs. Only her belly betrayed her, having lost the tautness of youth, and then there were the lines on her face, at the corner of her eyes and on her neck. Not so bad, she thought, touching her neck, if she was careful to keep her chin up.

A beautiful woman, Alicia Colbert—and her husband had not touched her in four years. He had a mistress—a string of mistresses—of that she was sure, and God help sometimes she wondered about Robert and Ana. It was horrible to think of your own daughter that way, but she would not have put it past Ana to seduce her own father. Hadn't Alicia caught her in bed with John when she was only thirteen? At sixteen John had already been larger than most men, in more ways than one, and Ana was always a curious little girl. Luckily, Alicia had interrupted them before much harm could be done. She could still see Ana leaning over her brother's huge penis, her tongue flicking over it . . . and the look of pure dumb pleasure on John's face . . .

Jesus, she thought, folding her arms around herself, if she had ever told Robert about that he'd have killed John, even though it had been John who had been the victim—although the poor, dumb boy never looked at it that way. He had never been able to figure out what he'd done wrong.

And Ana, even at thirteen, had been very well developed, taking after her mother in that way.

To Robert Ana was always an angel.

Only Alicia, her mother, saw her for the little vixen that she was.

If the gambler had killed her, Alicia thought, she had probably brought it on herself.

Still, she was her daughter, and she *should* be feeling some degree of grief.

Why wasn't she?

Maybe it was because the girl had brought her so much grief in life, she had none left for her in death.

Alicia put her dressing gown back on and went to bed.

She knew that Robert would not be joining her tonight. He hadn't slept with her since the death of Ana. They had shared a bed for the past four years without any sexual contact, but since the death of their daughter Robert had not even done that.

And God help, that made her wonder even more about the strange relationship between father and daughter.

A man, Alicia thought as she drifted off to sleep.

Maybe what I need is a man, a lover of my own.

She'd been remarkably faithful over the past four years. Maybe it was time she did something solely for herself, for a change.

EIGHT

Clint felt sorry for the clerk at the New Orleans House. He'd had to talk long and hard to convince the man that he was not switching hotels because of any deficiency in the service at the New Orleans House. The man had almost called for the manager to try to convince Clint to stay before Clint had finally slipped the man five dollars and left the hotel.

He walked the seven blocks to the Napoleon Hotel and checked in there. He still had not given the two men who attacked him a second thought.

The Napoleon was fancier than the New Orleans House, and more expensive. The clerk had a French accent, and the ambiance was so obviously French that Clint started wondering about the maids.

Well, he'd find that out soon enough.

Up in his new room, on the second floor overlooking the street, he thought about the two men. The attempt had been so badly bungled that he was almost sure they were amateurs. It had probably been their first robbery attempt. Still, he'd have to tell the chief about them tomorrow, just in case they decided to continue their little crime spree.

He sat on the bed and became aware of the growling noise in his stomach. He reminded himself that in the morning he'd have to move Duke to a livery stable closer to his new hotel. Right now he needed to get something to eat. He'd be able to think better on a full stomach.

He went downstairs to sample the Napoleon's dining room.

The food in the dining room was fair. For one thing it was a little too fancy for his tastes, with French names on the menu, and it was prepared in some kind of sauce he could have done without. Starting tomorrow he'd try to find a small café that served meat and potatoes the way he liked it. His tastes were simple and anything but fancy.

The coffee, at least, was strong, the way he liked it, and the company in the dining room was excellent.

It was past the dinner hour and there was only one other table that was occupied. Sitting at it was a strikingly pretty woman who appeared to be in her late twenties. She had auburn hair worn pulled back from her face so that Clint couldn't tell its exact length. Her face turned down most of the time, but he'd seen enough to know that she had full lips, a straight nose and large eyes. Her eyebrows were full and dark, which he found particularly appealing. She reminded him of Anne Archer, a lady bounty hunter he'd become quite fond of over the years since their first meeting.

He watched the woman while he ate. She was well dressed in an expensive-looking suit, obviously a guest since she wore no top clothes. She ate with very economical movements—that is, no wasted movement at all. She knew exactly what she wanted to do at every moment. There were no little half movements towards a water glass or a cup of coffee. She reached for everything with the same precision and assuredness.

He liked her, and wanted to meet her, but he felt guilty about approaching her. Justin was in jail, convicted of murder, and here he was eyeing a young lady in the hotel dining room.

Hell, he thought, if the tables were turned Justin would be doing the same thing.

Well, he was the first to admit that there were worlds of difference between himself and Justin Tarr, but they did have one thing in common.

They both loved women.

When the waiter came to his table he said, "Would you bring the young lady a glass of your best red wine?"

"But, monsieur," the waiter said, "she did not order any wine."

"No," Clint said, "I am ordering it for her."

"Ah," the sad-faced man said, "as a gift?"

"As a token," Clint said.

"Ah, oiu, monsieur," the waiter said, "I will bring her the token."

"Thank you."

"And for you, monsieur?"

"More coffee."

"Oiu, monsieur."

"Wait a minute," Clint said as the waiter turned away.

"Monsieur."

"Do you have any flowers in the hotel?"

"Oiu, monsieur."

"Any roses?"

"I can look, monsieur," the man said, with a shrug. "Perhaps."

"All right, if you do have a rose, bring her one with the glass of wine."

"Ah, another token, monsieur?"

"Yes," Clint said, "another token."

"At once, monsieur," the waiter said, seeming to get into the spirit of things.

The waiter went off and Clint watched the woman, hoping she wouldn't finish before the waiter returned. Her dinner check was already on her table and all she had to do, since she was a guest, was sign it and leave.

Luckily, before she could do so, the waiter arrived with the glass of wine. He also carried a single red rose in a small, long-necked vase. He had outdone himself.

Clint watched as the woman looked up in surprise, listened to what the waiter had to say, and then looked over at Clint. He waited to see if she was going to pick up the wine glass, and when she did he smiled and she returned the smile, and nodded.

She drank the wine, signed her check, and left the dining room without stopping by his table, or even looking at him again.

But he knew he'd gotten her.

She'd taken the rose with her.

As he left the dining room the waiter said, "Monsieur, she was very touched."

"I could see that," Clint said, wryly. "What's your name?"

"Richard."

"Thank you, Richard," Clint said, tipping the man handsomely.

"Monsieur," Richard said. Clint looked down at the object the waiter held in his hand. It was the woman's check.

Written on the check was her room number, 210, and she had signed her name with a flourish: Julie Graft.

"Thank you, Richard."

The waiter simply smiled and walked away.

NINE

Clint was reclining on his bed, clad only in his trousers, when there was a knock on the door. It was a firm knock, with nothing tentative about it.

He got up off the bed, considered for a moment his gun, which was hanging on the bedpost, then went to the door without it.

He opened it and found Julie Graft standing in the hall. She was holding the rose he'd sent her up to her nose.

"Let me explain myself before you say anything," she said.

"All right."

"You are the first interesting man I've met since I came to New Orleans."

"But we haven't—"

"I said wait!"

He put his hands up in an attitude of surrender and waited.

"A lot of men have approached me," she said, and he could see why. Up close she was even more striking. "I've received bouquets of flowers and bottles of champagne or wine, but you are the first to send me a single glass of wine and a single red rose."

"And you find that interesting?" he asked.

"Very," she said, putting her hand on his chest, "and now I think I would like to come in . . . if you don't mind, of course."

"I don't mind at all," he said.

She entered the room and closed the door behind her. She put her hand against his chest again and pushed, guiding him back to the bed. When they stopped she used the rose on him, running it down over his nose, his mouth, his chest, to his navel and finally stopping at his belt.

"This," she said, putting her hand on the belt, "has to go."

"Don't you want to know my name?" he asked.

"After," she said, coming close to him and kissing him deeply, wetly. "After," she said again, against his mouth.

Perhaps it was more the situation than anything else, but Clint found himself more excited by this woman than any in recent memory. In more ways than one she reminded him of Anne Archer, and perhaps that had something to do with it.

Anne was prettier, but Julie was bigger, and taller. They had the same color hair, the same dark eyebrows, but where Anne's lips were both full, Julie's lower lip was very lush, while the upper was not.

After they had undressed and settled down on the bed, he had chewed on her lower lip for a while, then switched his attention to her breasts, which were full and firm. Her nipples were dark brown, and he nursed each one in turn while she tangled her legs with his, rubbing her smooth thighs over his hairy ones.

Abruptly, she pushed him down on his back and kissed him. She kissed his mouth, his chin, his neck, his chest, licked *his* nipples—one of the few women he could recall having done that—and continued downward, over his belly and navel, through the tangle of hair until she encountered his erection, standing stiff and tall. She wrapped one hand around the base and licked the head with relish. She moaned then and took him in her mouth and he closed his eyes. Her mouth was incredibly hot and educated and in moments she had him swelling to the point of bursting. She abandoned him then, leaving him to grow cold as the air dried her saliva on him, and she began to kiss his thighs, nipping them from time to time, fondling his testicles with her left hand, still holding his penis with her right. He felt himself throbbing and wasn't at all sure that he wasn't going to ejaculate into the air—how high would it have gone?—but in the end was able to bring himself under control.

She moved over him then and mounted him, allowing him to slide into her ever so slowly. As hot as her mouth was, he now felt as if he were inside an oven.

She moved over him slowly, rubbing her breasts against his chest, moving her hips, squeezing him inside of her, sliding her hands beneath him to cup his buttocks.

Through all of this she hadn't muttered a word. She'd moaned, or groaned, but never spoke until they began to pound at each other and he finally exploded inside of her.

"Jesus . . . Moses!" she cried.

She used that same strange oath several times during the night, each time just before she climaxed.

Clint was on top of her at one point, driving into her, and as she opened her mouth to use the oath he silenced her with his own. He felt himself swell within her and then he began to ejaculate with more force than he could have imagined, considering how many times they had made love already that night. It was almost as painful as it was pleasurable, and as he rolled off of her he thought that perhaps he ought to give it a rest.

He woke with the first light and watched her dress. She did so quietly, assuming that he was still asleep, and he let her think so. He closed his eyes as she came to the bed, kissed him gently, and then started for the door.

"Adams," he said sleepily, as she reached it.

"What?" she asked, surprised.

"Clint Adams," he said.

She smiled and said, "Glad to meet you," and let herself out.

He was glad to have met her, too.

Almost.

TEN

Later that morning he once again presented himself at the New Orleans Police Department building, asking first for Inspector Chevalier.

"Inspector Chevalier is out, sir," the young officer manning the desk told him.

"So early?" Clint asked. He thought he'd gotten there early enough not to miss the man.

"The inspector is very dedicated, sir."

"So I see. May I see Chief Thoreau?"

"I'll check for you, sir."

"Thank you."

The officer checked and showed Clint into the chief's office.

"Good morning, Mr. Adams."

"Chief."

"May I offer you some coffee?"

"Please," Clint said. "I skipped breakfast hoping to

get here early enough to see Inspector Chevalier."

"Ah," the chief said, pouring a second cup from the pot on his desk, "and Emil is out?"

"It would appear so."

Handing Clint the cup of coffee, Thoreau said, "Emil is very dedicated."

"So I've been told."

"I have your friend's effects for you."

Effects, Clint thought. That makes him sound as if he was dead. Maybe to the chief's way of thinking, Justin already was dead.

"Where are they?"

"They will be waiting for you at the front desk after we have finished our little chat."

"Is that what we're having?"

"Well," the chief said, "I assumed that you would discover some other questions you'd like answered."

"One or two," Clint admitted.

"Such as?"

"Who defended Justin Tarr?"

"An attorney was appointed for him."

"Who?"

"His name is Carl Quincannon."

"He doesn't sound like a Cajun," Clint remarked.

"Not all of us are Cajun, Mr. Adams," the chief said. "I am not, for instance."

"And Inspector Chevalier?"

"Yes," Thoreau said, "Emil is from the bayou."

"Where can I find Mr. Quincannon?"

"He has an office in the center of the city. His name is on the window. You won't be able to miss it."

"I hope not. Is he competent?"

"As competent as any attorney," Thoreau said. "Believe me, Mr. Adams, your friend received a fair trial."

"Speaking of which," Clint said, "who were the witnesses against him?"

The chief pursed his lips and made a pyramid out of his hands.

"I'm afraid I can't tell you that."

"It will be a matter of record," Clint said. "I could look it up in the transcript."

"That may be so," the chief said, "and that is perhaps what you will have to do."

"You refuse to tell me?"

"I do."

Clint found this very curious, but decided not to push it. He could even find out from Justin, if need be.

"Very well," Clint said, "then I'll just make my report and be on my way."

"Report?" the chief asked, frowning.

"Yes," Clint said, "two rather inept men tried to rob me last night, after I left here."

"That's terrible," the chief said. "Make a report to Officer Hautala outside and we will try to bring them in."

"You shouldn't have much trouble," Clint said, standing up. "They really were amateurs."

"Nevertheless, they might try to rob someone else."

"They'll have to wait until the big one's wrist heals."

"His wrist?"

"Yes, the smaller man tried to brain me with a club and hit his partner instead."

"A big man, you say?"

"Very big," Clint said.

"I see," the chief said, lapsing into deep thought for a moment. "Very well," he said, rousing himself, "make your report and we will do our best."

"I couldn't ask for anymore than that," Clint said. "Good day, Chief."

"Good day, Mr. Adams."

The chief waited for Clint Adams to leave his office, closing the door behind him, and then he slammed his hand down on his desk and said, "The fools!"

At the front desk Clint made his report and then retrieved an envelope that supposedly held the property Justin had on him when he was arrested. He did not open the envelope there. He wanted to wait until he was in his room for that.

After leaving the station he went to the livery where he'd left Duke the day before, paid for a day's care and moved the big gelding to a stable closer to the Napoleon Hotel. After that he went looking for a restaurant where he could get a decent breakfast.

He cringed at the thought of what the Napoleon's cook could do to eggs.

ELEVEN

After breakfast Clint went looking for and found Carl Quincannon's office. The chief had been right. You couldn't miss the plate glass window with his name on it.

CARL QUINCANNON, ATTORNEY AT LAW it said, curving across the window in gold lettering.

The office was on the second floor of a building, over a hardware store. Clint looked for the entrance to the second floor and found it just off the corner of the building. There was another sign there with Quincannon's name on it, stuck to the wall. Clint mounted the steps and knocked on the door.

"Come in," a voice called.

Clint opened the door and stepped into utter chaos.

The office was a mess. There were files piled on tables, chairs, the floor, and in the midst of it all was a tall, gangly man with brown hair that fell across his eyes, wire-framed glasses, and large hands with knobby knuckles. He looked like a farmer, not a lawyer.

"Carl Quincannon?"

The man looked up from the stack of files he'd been regarding and squinted.

"That's me. Who are you?"

"My name is Clint Adams."

He studied Clint for a moment longer.

"Do I know you?" he finally asked.

"No."

"Do you need a lawyer?"

"No."

"Do I owe you money?"

"No."

"You're not an old client, or a prospective client, and you're not here to collect for someone I *do* owe money to?" Quincannon asked.

"No to all of that."

"What brings you here then, Mr. Adams?"

"I need to ask you some questions."

"About what?" He was holding a bunch of file folders and shifted his grip so they wouldn't slide out of his hands.

"Justin Tarr."

"That one!" he said.

All of the file folders he'd been holding went tumbling to the floor. When they struck they burst apart and papers flew all over.

"Oh, shit!" Quincannon said, glaring down at them. He looked up at Clint then and asked, "Do you want some coffee?"

"Always," Clint said.

"Let's get out of here."

TWELVE

Quincannon left dark, dusty fingerprints on the side of his cup as he lifted it to his mouth to drink his coffee.

He'd led Clint to a small café about two blocks from his office.

"I always come here when I want to get away from the mess," he said.

"Why don't you clean the mess?" Clint asked.

"I have been," Quincannon said, "for seven months." He put his cup down and said, "I'm getting closer, too."

Clint looked at the man and saw something he hadn't seen initially. He saw the steel gray eyes behind the man's glasses. They were strong eyes, steady as they stared at Clint, and probably steady when they stared at a judge or a jury.

"What can I do for you, Mr. Adams?"

"I'd like to know what happened to Justin Tarr."

"Pure and simple?"

"I'd prefer it that way."

"He was railroaded."

Clint waited.

"Do you know the term?"

"I do," Clint said. "It means he was innocent."

"Not necessarily," Quincannon said. "What it means is that he was convicted on the basis of phony evidence."

"Well, if you know that—"

"Ah!" Quincannon said, stopping Clint. "I know it, but I can't prove it."

"Well, maybe I can."

"Is that why you're here? Are you a private detective? A Pinkerton, or something?"

"No, nothing like that," Clint said. "I'm just a friend of Justin's who'd like to see him go free. Can we back up a little?"

"To where?"

"To where I said he was innocent and you said not necessarily. Do you think he's innocent?"

"All my clients are innocent, Mr. Adams."

"Look, could you try calling me Clint?"

"All right, Clint."

"Now could you try answering my question?"

"I thought I did."

"No, you gave me lawyerese," Clint said.

"You want people-ese?"

"I want a straight answer."

"All right," Quincannon said. "Yeah, I think Justin's innocent."

"Have you filed an appeal?"

"I have, but by the time we get it he could be hanged. You see, the judge is good friends with the Colberts."

"The Colberts?"

"Don't you know about the Colberts?"

"I know very little beyond the fact that Justin was convicted of killing a woman he says he never met."

"I can see I'm going to have to give you a history lesson," Quincannon said.

"Short and sweet, I hope."

Quincannon frowned and looked disappointed.

"Well, I was going to give you the long version, but okay, here's the short one. Robert Colbert is the father of the girl who was killed, Ana Colbert, and he is the most powerful man in New Orleans. Ergo, your friend was railroaded."

"What about the witness?"

Quincannon made a face.

"That's a tough one. The witness is a very respected member of this community."

"Who?"

"A woman named Louise Killough."

"What does she do?"

"She runs a hat shop."

"A hat shop?"

"Yep."

"And?"

"And . . . well, some people say that the hat shop was bought for her with Colbert money."

"By whom?"

"Robert."

"The father."

"Yes."

"She's his mistress?"

Quincannon looked around and said, "Nobody would ever dare say that in the open, but some say yes."

"And that makes her a reliable witness?"

"Her standing in the community made her a reliable witness, as far as the court was concerned."

"And nobody brought up in court that she was the mistress of the dead girl's father?"

"Jesus, no," Quincannon said, then grinned broadly and said, "Wouldn't it have been great if somebody had?"

"Why didn't you?" Clint asked. "You were supposed to be defending Justin."

"Hey, I defended him to the best of my ability, which is considerable, let me tell you."

"So what happened?"

"I told you, we were up against a stacked deck. There was never any doubt about the outcome."

"And you accepted that?"

"No. I told you I filed for an appeal."

"Oh, great."

"Well, what would you want me to do, go in with guns blazing and break him out? Maybe that's what you would do, being who you are."

"Being who I am?" Clint asked slowly.

"Well, you are, aren't you?"

"I are what?"

"Not what, who."

"All right, who am I?"

"The Gunsmith . . . aren't you? I mean, isn't that what they call you?"

"Some people call me that, yeah," Clint said, "but it's sort of the same as Mr. Colbert's mistress."

"What do you mean?"

"Nobody ever says it out in the open."

"Whoops," Quincannon said, "have I committed a *faux pas*?"

"A what?"

"That's Frenchie for a boo-boo."

Clint frowned and wondered if the man's eyes were lying to him.

"Mr. Quincannon—"

"Carl, please."

"Carl, if I can find you some hard evidence that Justin Tarr is *not* guilty, can you get him free?"

"With hard evidence?" Quincannon said. "I should be able to."

"What do you mean, you 'should' be able to?"

"You have to remember that we're dealing with the Colberts, here. They're a very powerful family."

"How many of them are there?"

"Lots."

"Let's stick to the immediate family."

"Well, there's Robert, his wife Alicia—a beautiful woman he treats like absolute shit—and then there's the two boys, Ethan and John."

"Ethan?" Clint said, the name ringing a bell. "One real big, one smaller and thinner—"

"That's them. Have you met them?"

"I have," Clint said. "One of them's got a broken wrist now."

"Oh yeah? Which one?"

"The big one."

Quincannon's eyes widened behind his glasses.

"You broke Johnny Colbert's wrist?"

"No, I didn't," Clint said, "his brother did."

"Wait a minute," Quincannon said, frowning. "Ethan broke John's wrist."

"Right."

"Why?"

"He was trying to club me and I moved."

"And what happened to Ethan?"

"I punched him in the nose—might have broken it, too."

"Oh Jesus," Quincannon said, "I miss all the good stuff. Tell me, why were the boys picking on you?"

"I thought they were trying to rob me, but now it's not hard to guess what they wanted."

"What?"

"To run me out of New Orleans."

"Why—oh. Because you're here to help your friend?"

"That's right," Clint said, pushing his chair back.

"How did they know you were even here?"

"That's what I intend to find out," Clint said, standing up.

"And how are you going to do that?"

"With your help."

"What can I do?"

Clint looked at him and said, "Just point me in the direction of the Colberts."

THIRTEEN

The house the Colberts called home was impressive, even intimidating—although Clint assumed that was one of the desired reactions. People who live in ostentatious homes such as this one lived to intimidate people who couldn't afford homes like it.

He knocked on the huge white door and waited patiently. In a home this size it would take some time for the door to be answered.

Finally, the door was opened by an attractive black maid who simply stared at Clint, waiting for him to speak.

"I'd like to see Mr. Colbert."

"He not home."

"Mrs. Colbert, then."

"I ask. What your name?"

"Adams, Clint Adams."

"Wait here."

She closed the door in his face and again he put his patience to work. Finally, the door was opened again, this time by an extremely attractive woman in her mid- to late-forties. Clint immediately appreciated the woman's beauty and felt that it might even have been enhanced by her age. If this was the dead girl's mother, he could imagine what the girl must have looked like.

"Mrs. Colbert?"

She was staring at him and he had to say her name again before she spoke. He got the distinct impression that she was admiring him as much as he was admiring her. He reminded himself that she was not that much older than he was.

"Yes, I'm sorry," she said. "Is there something I can help you with?"

"A couple of things, yes," he said. "May I come in?"

"My husband is not home—"

"Are your sons home?"

"My sons? Why no, they're not."

"I'd like to talk to you about them."

"What's happened—"

"May I come in?" he asked again.

"Yes . . . please," she said, backing up to admit him. She closed the door and said to him, "This way."

He followed her, admiring the way her body moved inside her simple dress. She had full breasts that were surprisingly firm for her age.

She led him to a sitting room, but did not offer him a seat.

"What is this about my sons?"

"I had a little altercation with them last night."

"Oh," she said, "that was you?"

"Yes. I'm sorry, but I reported it to the police. I thought they were trying to rob me. I can see now that was a mistake on my part." He used his hands to indicate that the house was his reason for saying that.

"Yes, they'd have no need to rob anyone," she said. "As a matter of fact, my husband and my sons are at the police station now. They must be clearing that matter up. Will you, uh, be pressing charges?"

"I don't think so," he said. "They seem to have come out on the bad end of the exchange."

"Yes, I would agree. I must thank you for your . . . understanding."

"Well, that's just it, Mrs. Colbert," he said, "I don't understand. Why would they attack me that way, without provocation?"

She frowned, then shook her head as if to dispel some errant thought.

"I'm sorry, Mr. Adams, but why are you here—in New Orleans, I mean?"

"I'm here to help a friend who's in trouble."

"This friend," she said, "would that be the man who killed my daughter?"

"The man who was arrested for killing your daughter, yes, ma'am."

"Please," she said, closing her eyes, "don't call me ma'am."

"I'm sorry, ma—uh—"

"My name is Alicia."

"Mrs. Colbert—"

"I wish you would use my name, Mr. Adams," she said. "Would you like something to drink? I can have Samantha get you—"

"Nothing to drink, thank you, Mrs.—I mean, Alicia.

I'm sorry, Alicia, but I'm not convinced that my friend Justin Tarr did kill your daughter."

"I don't understand," she said. "He was tried and convicted. There was an eyewitness—"

"A questionable eyewitness at best—wouldn't you agree, Alicia?"

"I . . . don't know what you mean."

"I think you do."

There was an awkward silence then, finally broken by Alicia Colbert.

"If you are referring to the fact that the witness is a . . . friend of my husband's—" She stopped then, looking annoyed, whether at him or at herself—or her husband—he couldn't be sure. "Oh hell," she said. She walked to a small sideboard and poured herself a stiff glass of brandy.

"Would you like a brandy?"

"Yes, that would be fine."

She poured him one and brought it to him. When he reached for it their hands touched and there was an unmistakable surge of attraction. He'd felt it at the door, and he felt it even more now. She was a lovely, undoubtedly experienced woman with a strong physical presence. Why Robert Colbert would need to turn to a mistress he didn't understand. Then again, he had not seen the mistress.

"I called Louise Killough a friend of my husband's," she said. "Well, everyone in town knows that she is his mistress, the latest in a long line of mistresses."

"May I say that makes him a fool in my book?"

She inclined her head at the compliment and said, "You may. It's nice to hear. In any case, the fact that she is my husband's mistress doesn't necessarily make her a questionable witness . . . does it?"

"It does to me, Alicia," Clint said. "At the very least, it raises some question in my mind. I intend to talk to Miss Killough about it."

"You're an attractive man, Mr. Adams—" she said.

"Clint, please."

"Clint . . ." she said, pausing. "Yes, a very attractive man. I would be very careful with Louise Killough if I were you. She likes two kinds of men, the rich kind and the attractive kind."

"And which does she prefer?"

"Why, the rich kind, of course. That's why she has latched onto my husband."

"And why has your husband latched onto her? You'll excuse me, Alicia, but you are a beautiful woman. Why would your husband—"

"There are personal problems involved," she said. "I'm sure you're not interested in hearing them."

She put her empty glass down and looked him square in the eye.

"I will have a talk with my sons, Clint. They won't be bothering you anymore."

"Excuse me again, Alicia, but who has more influence with your sons, you or your husband?"

She bit her lip for a moment—something Clint felt like doing at that moment, biting *her* lip—and said, "You're quite right in assuming that my husband does. Also, he may have sent them after you yesterday. I wouldn't put it past him."

"Alicia," he said, putting his own empty glass down, "will I be able to talk to your husband, at all?"

"About Ana's death? I think not," Alicia said, shaking her head. "He was crushed by our daughter's death, Clint, and as far as he's concerned Justin Tarr killed her. I don't think he would talk to you."

"Well, I hope you understand that I have no desire to see the killer of your daughter go unpunished; I'm just not sure they have the right man for it. I intend to look into the matter and see what I can find out."

"I hope you'll keep me informed, Clint," she said. "We would have to meet secretly, of course . . ."

"Of course . . ."

"I'll walk you out."

They walked to the front door side by side, and Clint could feel the sexual tension in the air. He wondered how long it had been since Alicia Colbert had slept with her husband—or any man, for that matter.

At the door she extended her hand and he took it. They stood that way for a few moments and she said, "Will you keep me informed?"

"I will," he said, releasing her hand. "I promise."

She opened the door for him and he left. He didn't look back and heard the door close behind him. He continued on without looking behind him.

After Clint Adams left, Alicia Colbert put her back to the closed door and tried to regulate her breathing. She had found him *extremely* attractive, and wondered at the coincidence of meeting such a man just the day after she'd made the decision to take a lover. She'd had several men in mind from town, some younger—some *considerably* younger—and some older, some her own age, but none of them appealed to her now that she had met Clint Adams.

Of course, the fact that Robert would go crazy if he

ever found out that she was sleeping with the man who was trying to free the man *he* thought killed their daughter—well, that was icing on the cake.

She decided that the day wouldn't pass without her seeing Clint Adams again.

FOURTEEN

After leaving Alicia Colbert, Clint had a couple of options. He could have gone to the police station to see Colbert and his sons, and the chief, but instead he decided to go and see Louise Killough while Robert Colbert was otherwise occupied. If Colbert would refuse to talk to him, he was going to have to give the man a good reason to change his mind.

Carl Quincannon had told him where Louise Killough's hat shop was, so he went directly to that part of the city that held many of the little shops that women would frequent and found it tucked in between a dress shop and an ice cream parlor.

As he entered the shop a little bell rang over his head, announcing his arrival. There were several women in the store and they all turned at the sound and stared at him. Two of them were fifty or better, the other—possibly the daughter of one of the others—was about seventeen and pretty. She stared at Clint until one of the other women tugged on her arm, forcing her to turn around.

The woman behind the counter stared at Clint and there was no one to tug on her arm. She was in her late twenties, a tall, slender, classically beautiful woman with an impressive mane of blonde hair.

Clint looked around a bit until one woman left, and then the other, with the seventeen-year-old girl in tow. She sneaked another look at Clint as she went out the door behind her mother, and he gave her a smile and a tip of his hat.

"We don't get many men in here. Don't tell me," Louise Killough said from behind him, "you're looking for a hat for your wife."

"I'm not married," he said, turning and looking at her. She was still standing behind the counter, but her right hand was toying with her hair, a sure sign that a woman was going to become flirtatious.

"Oh," Louise Killough said, "then for a lady friend?"

"Just got into town yesterday."

"Well," she said, "a man as attractive as you are, that would be plenty of time to find a lady friend."

"Maybe," he said, "if I didn't have something else on my mind."

"Oh? And what would that be?"

"Murder."

Her hand dropped from her hair and her face was stiff.

"Pardon?" she said.

"I said murder, specifically the murder of a young woman named Ana Colbert."

"I don't want to talk about that."

"You *were* the prime witness at the trial, weren't you?" he asked.

"I'm not supposed to—I don't want to talk about it," she stammered.

"Who told you that you weren't supposed to talk about it?" he asked. "The judge—or Robert Colbert?"

"Who are you?" she asked. "What do you want?"

"My name is Clint Adams, and I'm here to see that the person who really killed Ana Colbert doesn't get away with it."

"They have the man who killed her."

"I don't think so."

Nervously she said, "He was convicted."

"On your testimony."

"There were others who testified."

"Don't be modest, Louise," he said. "It was your testimony that did the trick. I'll bet you were coached real well, too."

"I can't—" she started to say.

"I know, you're not supposed to talk about it."

"No . . . I don't *want* to talk about it."

"Well, I'll bet that's true, too, but you really were instructed not to talk about it, weren't you?"

"Look, Mr.—"

"Adams, Clint Adams," he said. "Remember my name. You'll want to tell your lover, Colbert, that I was here. He'll want to know my name. Tell him that if he wants to talk to me he shouldn't send his sons. Tell him to do his own dirty work, next time."

He moved towards the door, then stopped and looked at her again. She was still standing stiffly behind the counter.

"It was a pleasure meeting you, Louise," he said. "We'll be talking again."

He left, knowing that he'd sufficiently rattled her to the point where she'd be looking for Robert Colbert—and Colbert would be looking for him.

He went back to his hotel, so that the man would be able to find him.

After Clint left the hat shop Louise Killough hurried out from behind the counter, locked the door and turned her CLOSED sign out. She hurried to the back room then and sat for a moment, wondering what she should do.

Robert had promised her that this would never happen. He had promised that no one would ever dare question her testimony—and now this Clint Adams was there, looking at her like he *knew* she'd lied on the stand, and telling her that they would talk again.

In the end, panic-stricken, she did just what Clint Adams had hoped she would do.

She left the shop by the back door and went looking for Robert Colbert.

FIFTEEN

When Robert Colbert returned home after straightening out the mess his sons had made with the law, Alicia Colbert took perverse pleasure in informing him of Clint Adams's visit to their home.

"What?" Colbert roared. "He came here?"

"He did."

"What did he want?"

"To talk to you."

"What did you tell him."

"Nothing."

"Alicia—"

"I told him you weren't home."

"Did you tell him where I was?"

"I did."

"And what did he say?"

"That he wouldn't press charges against the boys."

Colbert frowned.

"How did you convince him to do that?"

"He's a very reasonable man."

"Reasonable!" he exploded. "He's trying to get my daughter's killer free, and you call him reasonable?"

"*Our* daughter, Robert," she corrected him, but he ignored her.

"The man had the nerve to come to my home," he said. He looked at her again and said, "What else did you tell him, Alicia?"

"I told him that the boys made a mistake, and that it wouldn't happen again."

"You're damned right it won't," Colbert said. "I'll send professionals this time, and not those bunglers."

"Robert—"

"Did he say where he was going from here?"

This is going to be the best part, Alicia Colbert thought with great satisfaction.

"Yes."

"Where?"

"He said he was going to see Louise Killough."

"What?"

Colbert grabbed his wife by the shoulders and squeezed so tightly that she knew she'd have bruises when he let her go.

"You told him about Louise Killough?"

"I did not," she said, determined not to let the pain she was feeling show on her face. "He brought her name up himself."

"And what did you tell him?"

"Robert," she said, "let me go."

Colbert hesitated a moment, then released her and stepped back. She wouldn't rub her shoulders until he left the house.

"What did you tell him about Louise?"

"I refused to discuss . . . her, especially in my own house. Just as I refuse to discuss her now."

If there had been a knock on the door neither of them had heard it, but Samantha, the black maid, came to the sitting room door and said, "Mr. Colbert?"

"Yes, Samantha?"

"Someone to see you."

"Who is it?"

Samantha looked first at Mrs. Colbert, and then at Mr. Colbert before saying, "It Louise Killough, suh."

Colbert turned and looked at her.

"Take her to my study."

"I won't have that woman in my house, Robert!" Alicia Colbert shouted.

He turned and glared at her.

"Your house, woman? *I* built this house."

"If you bring that woman into this house," Alicia said evenly, "I will kill her."

"Alicia."

"She will not leave this house alive, Robert. I promise you."

Colbert studied his wife for a few moments, and decided that she was telling the truth.

"All right," he conceded, "all right." He turned to Samantha and said, "Ask Miss Killough to wait outside for me."

"Yes, suh."

As the maid left Colbert pointed the index finger of his right hand at his wife and said, "You will not talk to this man Adams again, do you understand?"

"I understand, Robert," she said meekly.

"I don't know if I will be home for dinner, Alicia."

"I will try to console myself," she said.

He stared at her, was about to say something, then thought better of it and left.

She almost wished that he *had* tried to bring Louise Killough into the house.

She would gladly have blown the woman's head off with a shotgun.

"Why did you keep me waiting out here?" Louise Killough demanded when Robert Colbert appeared.

"Alicia wouldn't have you in the house," he said.

"*She* wouldn't have—"

"Never mind that," he said, grabbing her arm in a painful grip. "Did Adams come to see you?"

"That's why I'm here," she said. "He knows I lied, Robert—"

"Shhh!" he said, shushing her sharply. "Don't *ever* say that!"

She lowered her voice and said, "He knows, damn it. You promised no one would question me—"

"I'll take care of Mr. Adams, Louise. Don't worry about it."

"I *am* worried about it, Robert!"

"Well don't be!" he said. "What did he say?"

"He said that we'd talk again."

"What did he say about *me!*"

"He said that next time you were to do your own dirty work. He said if you want to talk to him not to send your sons."

"That bastard!" Colbert said. "I'll show him some dirty work."

"Robert," Louise said, all of her anger fading as fear took over, "what's going to happen?"

"Never mind, Louise," he said, patting her arm now instead of gripping it. "Just go back to your shop."

"Robert—"

"Do as I say, Louise! I'll come by later tonight for dinner."

"I'm frightened, Robert."

"Damn it, woman!" he snapped. "Show some backbone!"

She stiffened then and said, "It's not my backbone you're interested in, Robert!"

He looked at her then and thought, no, it certainly isn't. It's your fine body, and your hair, and your wonderfully educated mouth, your youth, your vitality. . .

"All right, Louise," he said. "I apologize. Go back to your shop and I'll be by later."

She looked doubtful, but finally obeyed and started back to her shop.

Robert Colbert had an office in town, and that's where he headed.

He'd show this Clint Adams what *real* dirty work was!

SIXTEEN

Clint waited at his hotel for two hours and finally decided that Robert Colbert wasn't coming—at least, not himself. He decided to go down to the dining room and try lunch.

Hell, how bad could it be?

As he entered the busy dining room he saw Julie Graft seated at a table. She looked up as he entered, smiled and waved him over.

"Join me for lunch," she said.

"Now I'm glad I came down here," he said, sitting opposite her.

"Why?"

"The food here doesn't inspire me."

"But I do?" she asked.

"Exactly."

She smiled again and said, "Then why don't we skip lunch?"

"Now that sounds like a fine idea."

They spent the next hour in bed, skipping lunch, and managed to work up an appetite.

She'd said, "Jesus, Moses!" three times during the hour, and he was no longer able to hold back his question.

"Julie."

"What?" she asked, still naked to the waist as he watched her dress.

"I've only heard one other person say 'Jesus, Moses,'" he said. "Does that particular oath run in your family?"

"Sort of."

"What does 'sort of,' mean?" he asked.

She straightened up and stared at him. He also felt as if her brown nipples were staring at him.

"Why are you asking?"

"Well, the last person I heard say that was trying to take my head off."

"Who was that?"

"A side of beef named John Colbert."

"Well," she said, "that explains it, doesn't it?"

"Explains what?"

"John Colbert is my cousin."

"You're a Colbert?"

"Not quite," she said. "Could we talk about this over lunch?"

He swung his legs off the bed and said, "Why not?"

•   •   •

"My father is Alicia Colbert's brother," she said. "We left New Orleans when I was five, and I've returned now because—well, my father died recently."

"And your mother?"

"She died years ago."

"I'm sorry. Why are you here, exactly?"

"Well, Aunt Alicia and Uncle Robert, and their sons, are the only family I have, and I felt a need to be near my family."

"And?"

"The bastard won't even let me in his house!"

"The bastard being Robert Colbert?"

"Yes," she said, looking down at her plate, "he thinks I'm here looking for money—and I'm not." She looked up at him, her face hopeful, "Really, I'm not."

"I believe you," he said. "Tell me, how long have you been here?"

"A month."

"That long?"

"I . . . don't have any place else to go. I'm waiting a respectable time after Ana's death to try to talk to him again."

"Did you know Ana?"

"Not until I came here. She was born after we left."

"But you met her when you came here?"

"Yes," she said, "in fact, she and Aunt Alicia were the only ones who would talk to me."

"You became friends with Ana?"

"Hardly," she said. She picked up a spoon and stirred her coffee, which was odd because she drank it black with no sugar, the way he did. It was just something to do while she formed her thoughts.

"She was a little bitch," she said, finally, "and an outrageous flirt—oh, I hate to speak ill of the dead."

"Before you go any further, Julie," Clint said, "there's something you should know."

"What?"

He explained briefly his reason for being in New Orleans.

"That can't make you very popular with Uncle Robert," she said when he was done.

"The question is, what does it do to my popularity with you?"

She paused only a moment before saying, "No harm. I told you, I didn't like Ana, and besides, I don't think your friend did it, either."

"Why?" he asked, jumping at the remark.

"I don't think he knew her."

"Can you say for sure he didn't?"

"No, not for sure—"

"Were you allowed to testify at the trial?"

"No one asked me."

"Did you talk to Justin's attorney?"

"No . . . I guess I should have."

"That's all right. Would you be willing to do so now?"

"Sure, if you think it will do any good."

"I'll introduce you to him," he said. "It certainly can't do any harm."

"Have you talked to Aunt Alicia?"

"I have. She seemed reasonable enough."

"She is. It was she who told me not to leave town, that she would talk to my uncle. What about my cousins?"

"Yes," he said, "I've spoken with them." He was even more brief in outlining his encounter with them.

"Yes, they are morons," she said, "especially John, but he has an excuse. He's naturally stupid. Ethan seems to work at it. Do you know that he tried—well . . ."

"Tried what?"

"He was one of the men I told you about, the ones who didn't interest me."

"He tried to approach you—"

"He tried to force himself on me. I had to put my knee to good use to get away from him."

In his mind's eye Clint could see Julie kneeing Ethan between the legs, and he laughed.

"I'm sorry," Clint said, "even the hint of incest isn't funny."

"It certainly isn't. I told him in no uncertain terms that I wasn't interested, and he told me to leave town before I got hurt."

"Has he tried—"

"No, that encounter took place just before Ana was killed. I haven't seen Ethan or John since then."

"Julie . . . I'm sorry, tell me if I should mind my own business, but it seems to me any place would be better than here, with that family."

"I suppose it would," she said. "You see, I was devoted to my father and I've never lived on my own." She gave him a shy look and said, "That was one of the reasons I came to your room last night. I wanted to do something . . . oh, on my own, something . . . daring."

"You're not sorry, are you?"

"Oh, no."

"Good. Everyone should do something daring every so often."

"Have you?"

He laughed, because she had no idea of his reputation.

"In my case it's called doing something stupid, on occasion."

She frowned, not knowing whether to laugh or not.

"I don't understand."

"I'll explain some other time," he said. "Let's finish this . . . whatever it's called, and we'll go and see Carl Quincannon, Justin's lawyer."

Staring at his plate Clint thought that if he ever found himself in France, he'd probably starve to death.

SEVENTEEN

Clint knocked on Quincannon's door but there was no answer. He put his ear to the door and could hear Quincannon inside, muttering.

"He's here," he said. "He's engrossed in his filing."

Clint opened the door and knocked over a stack of files that had been set right against it.

"Shit!" Quincannon said.

"This is filing?" Julie asked.

Clint pushed the door open, doing more damage to the files.

"Sorry, Carl."

"Forget it," Quincannon said. "This place is a hopeless mess. Who's this?"

He was standing, tall and gangly, among stacks of files, staring at Julie. Clint thought for sure that he was smitten.

"This is Julie Graft," Clint said, "she's—"

"Oh, sure," Quincannon said, "the Colbert cousin."

"You know about her?" Clint asked.

"What's to know?" the lawyer said. "Hi, I'm Carl Quincannon."

"Nice to meet you," Julie said. They were too far away from each other to do more than nod.

"What else do you know about her?" Clint asked.

"Aside from the obvious—that she's real pretty—not much."

Quincannon seemed embarrassed at having complimented Julie, and Clint assumed that the lawyer was not exactly a ladies' man.

"Tell him, Julie."

"What's to tell?" she said. "I simply told Clint that I don't believe Justin Tarr even knew Ana Colbert."

"Well, that's fine," Quincannon said, looking down at the files spread out on the floor. "Do you see a file with the name Willis on it?"

Julie looked down and said, "Sure, here."

She picked up the file and, stretching so that she could reach, handed it to him.

"Is that all you have to say?" Clint asked.

"About what?" Quincannon asked.

"About what she just told you."

The lawyer looked at Clint and pushed his glasses further up on his nose. His finger left a smudge on his nose.

"She doesn't believe Tarr knew the dead girl. That's fine. I don't think he did, either. Trouble is, I couldn't prove it, and I'll bet she can't, either."

Clint looked at Julie, who shrugged helplessly.

"Quincannon," Clint said, "what do I have to bring you for you to be able to keep Tarr from being hanged?"

"Proof," Quincannon said, "hard evidence."

"When is he scheduled to be hanged?"

"Four days," Quincannon said. "You've got four days to get me something."

"What about his appeal?"

"When the judge is in somebody's pocket," the lawyer said, "an appeal can get lost in the shuffle of paperwork very easily."

"Jesus," Clint said.

"You don't have an easy job, my friend," Quincannon said.

"We," Clint said.

"We?" Quincannon said.

"We don't have an easy job," Clint said. "As far as I know, you're still Justin's attorney."

"Well, technically," Quincannon said.

"What do you mean, technically?"

"Well, I was assigned by the court," Quincannon said, "for the duration of the trial."

"But you filed for an appeal."

"That's a matter of course, Clint. What I'm saying is, I defended Tarr, but I was actually working for the state of Louisiana." He pronounced it "Loo-siana."

"So what you're saying is, if Tarr pays you then you'll be working for him."

"Right."

"Then consider yourself retained."

"I'll need a retainer," Quincannon said.

"Trust me for it," Clint said.

Quincannon looked at Clint, then Julie, then Clint again, then shrugged and said, "Hell, why not?"

"Where does the appeal go?" Clint asked.

"The capital," Quincannon said, "Baton Rouge."

"Well, pack a bag," Clint said, "you're headed for Baton Rouge."

"That's a hundred miles!" Quincannon complained.

"All the more reason you should start right away," Clint said. "You've got to get back here in four days with a stay of execution. Talk to the damned governor, if you have to."

"And who's gonna file?" Quincannon said.

Clint looked around and said, "A good stiff wind could file better than you."

Before Quincannon could reply Julie said, "I'll take care of it."

"You will?" the lawyer said.

"Sure, I used to handle my father's files. I'll have it all filed by the time you get back."

"Okay?" Clint said to Quincannon.

The lawyer shrugged his bony shoulders, brushed a lock of hair out of his face—leaving a couple of smudge marks on his forehead—and said, "Hell, yes."

EIGHTEEN

Robert Colbert sat in his town office, above the bank that he owned. Upon entering the building he had told his assistant, Frank Marlowe, "Get me Proffit."

Now Colbert was waiting for Douglas Proffit to arrive.

Proffit was Colbert's personal right hand, when it came to anything troublesome. He was a violent man who wrapped his violence in a facade of sophistication. Anyone looking at the man would think of an educated man, possibly a banker. He was hardly a banker, as he traded not in money, but in pain.

There was a knock at the door and Colbert called out, "Come!"

Frank Marlowe, a tall, slender young man who Colbert had constantly been pushing on Ana as a prospective husband, entered and said, "Proffit is here, sir."

"Send him in, Frank."

"Yes, sir."

Marlowe withdrew and Proffit appeared at the door. As usual he was impeccably dressed in black. His hair, as black as night, was slicked back, accentuating the widow's peak in front. He had long sideburns and a carefully trimmed mustache.

"You wanted me, Mr. Colbert?"

"Are you busy at the moment, Proffit?"

Proffit approached the desk and sat opposite Colbert. He removed black leather gloves and held them in one hand.

"I'm never too busy to do a job for you, Mr. Colbert," he said, "you know that."

"This may or may not be something you'll want to handle personally, Proffit," Colbert said.

"Tell me about it."

That night Julie took Clint to the French Quarter for dinner.

"This is not a good idea," Clint said for the third time in as many minutes. "I just don't like French food."

"Not the way they serve it at the hotel," she said. "Besides, this is not going to be French food, it's going to be Cajun food."

"What do you know about Cajun food?"

"It's the one thing I remember from my childhood," she said, "that I loved Cajun food."

She took him to a restaurant she said she had discovered her first week there, and ordered Cajun chicken with dirty rice.

"Dirty rice?" Clint asked.

"You'll see."

He did. The rice was sort of a brownish color, actually *looked* dirty, and yet he found it delicious, as he did the chicken—although the chicken was spicy.

"That's worse than Mexican food," he said, washing down the first bite with some ice water.

"You should drink hot coffee with it, not cold water," she said.

He tried that and found that it worked. Actually, once he got into the meal he didn't need to chase the hot chicken down with anything, anymore, and actually ate more.

After dinner they strolled the streets, listening to the music that was wafting out to the streets from some of the restaurants and clubs.

"It's a beautiful city," Clint said.

Julie had her arm linked through his.

"I wouldn't mind living here," she said, "if I could afford it."

"That shouldn't depend on Robert Colbert opening his home to you."

"I don't want to live with him," she said, "I just want him to acknowledge me as family."

"You think that will open some doors for you?"

"I'm not looking for someone to open doors for me, either," Julie said.

"What are you looking for?"

"I'm not sure," she admitted. "I guess I just want to think I still have family, somewhere."

"As far as living here, you could get a job," Clint said.

"Doing what?"

"Well . . . how well can you file? Maybe Quincannon will hire you?"

"Him?" she said, laughing. "He'd misplace me somewhere in that office."

"Not if you kept the office neat. Think about it."

"There's nothing for me to think about unless Quincannon offers me the job—on his own," she added, jerking on his arm. "I don't want anyone putting pressure on him."

"Why not?" he asked. "He may be too befuddled by you to think of it."

"Befuddled?"

"I guess you didn't notice the effect you had on him?"

"What effect? Try telling me he's not always that confused."

"No, he's confused all right, as far as I can see," Clint said. "I only met him myself yesterday, but I think he became even more confused when he saw you."

"I think you're imagining things," she said. "Maybe you're trying to get rid of me?"

"Rid of you?"

She immediately seemed embarrassed by her own remark, which she felt had been ill advised. She didn't want Clint Adams to think that she was laying some sort of claim to him already.

"I didn't—I don't mean you owe me anything—I mean, not that we're . . . involved or anything . . ." she stammered.

"Take it easy, Julie," he said, patting her hand, trying to put her at ease. "We like each other. That's enough, isn't it?"

"Yes," she said, seeming relieved that he wasn't annoyed with her. "Yes, that's more than enough. I need someone to like right now. Someone to talk to."

"I'm right here, Julie," he said, "even if you only want to talk."

"I know," she said, squeezing his arm, "I know, and I'm thankful."

"Why don't we get back to the hotel?" he asked, putting his arm around her.

"All right."

"I need to get some sleep," he said. "I don't have much time if I'm going to clear Justin Tarr."

When Clint and Julie returned to the hotel they parted company in the lobby. Julie understood Clint's need for some rest, and further wanted to demonstrate that she was not laying claim to any hold on him—certainly not after only one day.

"What about breakfast?" she asked.

"I don't know, Julie," Clint said. "I want to get a real early start."

"What are you going to do first?"

"I'm going to have to try talking to Louise Killough again."

"The mistress."

"Yes, and the main witness against Justin. If I can get her to admit that she lied, that might be all I'll need," Clint said.

"Well, good luck," she said, "and good night."

"I'll see you tomorrow, maybe in the afternoon."

She kissed him on the cheek and went up to her room. Clint waited in the lobby a few moments because he didn't trust himself to walk her to the room and then return to his own room immediately.

When he went up to his room he noticed a line of light beneath the door as he approached his room. Maybe Robert Colbert had decided to come and see him after all.

Clint didn't draw his gun, because he'd be able to get

it out in a hurry if he needed it. He put his key in the door and swung it open.

There was a Colbert in his room all right, but it wasn't Robert.

It was Alicia.

NINETEEN

"Good evening," he said.

She was sitting on his bed, fully dressed, with her hands in her lap. She looked uncomfortable at being there.

"Good evening," she said.

He closed the door and regulated the flame on the lamp, which she had set too high.

"What can I do for you tonight, Mrs. Colbert?"

"I think you know," she said.

Clint thought he knew, too, because the sexual tension was in the air even now.

"Do you think this is wise?" Clint asked. "What if someone saw you come up here?"

"I wouldn't care," she said, "but no one saw me."

"How did you get into the room?"

She smiled and said, "You don't know this, but my

husband owns this hotel. I have a skeleton key that fits every room."

"Nice," he said, "do you use it often?"

She gave him a very serious look and said, "I have never used this key before."

He believed her.

"Look, Mrs. Colbert—"

"Alicia."

"All right, Alicia, I just don't think this is a very wise move. For one thing, I've become friends with your niece, Julie."

"Julie's a nice girl," she said. "It's too bad for her that she's part of this family."

"She deserves better treatment than she's been getting," Clint said.

"I agree, but I don't see that as a reason I shouldn't be here."

"Well, how about the fact that I'm trying to clear the man who has been convicted of killing your daughter?"

"No," she said.

"Alicia."

She stood up and said, "If you want me to leave, I will."

It was a tough decision, and she proceeded to make it even tougher.

"But first I'd like you to know what you'll be missing."

She had a thigh-length coat on, which she removed to reveal a simple dress beneath it. She unbuttoned that and shrugged it from her shoulders, showing herself to be naked beneath it.

"I'm rather proud of the way I've kept my body, Clint," she said.

He could see why. Her breasts were full and firm, with very little hint of sag. Her nipples were pink and already distended with excitement.

"I also don't lie about my age," she said. "I'm forty-eight years old."

He wet his lips and said, "I'm impressed."

"I hoped you would be," she said, "but do you want me to leave?"

Yes, he thought.

"No," he said.

He could see that he wasn't going to get the rest tonight that he'd hoped for.

She was desperate.

She wanted to taste every inch of him, and wanted him to do the same to her.

"It's been so long," she kept saying as they made love, and experiencing her desperation and her ferocity Clint's belief that she hadn't been with a man in a long time was strengthened.

At first she demanded to be on top. She wanted him to suck her breasts as she rode his rigid cock, then she wanted to be on the bottom while he plowed her mercilessly.

"Harder!" she kept demanding, "Oh, harder!"

After that she got down on all fours on the bed and implored him to take her from behind. He was impressed by her firm ass, which could have belonged to a twenty-eight year old instead of a forty year old.

In fact, he was impressed by her energy and her stamina, but perhaps abstinence had fueled her for a full, active night.

● ● ●

"Jesus," he said sometime later, "you make *me* feel old."

They were both covered with perspiration and he could see that she was breathing as hard as he was.

"You make me feel young," she said. "I needed this very badly."

"Well," he said, "I'm glad I was around."

"So am I," she said. "It seems too much of a coincidence."

"What does?"

"I had just decided, after years of watching my husband's procession of mistresses, to take a lover of my own, and there you were."

"I was there for my own reasons."

"I realize that," she said, "but I hope you don't mind being used for my own reasons."

"If I did," Clint said, "I would have asked you to leave."

"I'm glad you didn't," she said. After a beat she said, "Have you slept with Julie?"

"Yes," he replied without hesitation. He waited for her to ask him to make some comparison, but she never did.

Instead, she wanted to make love again.

TWENTY

Later, as she dressed, he asked her, "Alicia, can we talk about Ana?"

Alicia Colbert paused a moment, then said, "Yes."

"Who do you think killed her?"

"I . . . don't know."

"Let me rephrase that," Clint said. "Do you think Justin Tarr killed her?"

"I don't know."

"Did she know him?"

"I don't know."

Frustrated, Clint said, "What do you know, Alicia?"

Fully dressed now she faced him.

"I didn't know my daughter very well, Clint, not for many years now. We weren't . . . close, not as friends, and not as mother and daughter."

"She was closer to her father, then?"

She hesitated a moment then said, "*He* was closer to

her. I don't know how close she felt to him, but he doted on her."

"Then he would probably know for sure whether or not she even knew Tarr?"

"I would think so, yes," she said. "He sometimes had someone keep an eye on her."

"Who?"

"Just a man who works for him," she said.

"What's the man's name?"

"Marlowe," she said. "He works for my husband at his bank. I think Robert even wanted Ana to get to know Frank Marlowe better."

"Was Marlowe in love with your daughter?"

"I don't know if anyone was in love with her," she said. "A lot of men *wanted* her."

"What about your sons?"

"What about them?"

"Forgive me . . . but would one of them have had any reason to kill her?"

"Not . . . that way."

"What way?"

"With a knife."

That startled Clint a little. What kind of a detective was he when he hadn't even asked to this point how the girl had been killed? He had taken it for granted that Justin hadn't killed her, and hadn't even asked the method that had been used.

"If John had killed her it would have been with his hands," she said, "and probably an accident. He doesn't know his own strength, sometimes. He's not . . . very smart, you know."

"I've noticed." Clint felt that there was more wrong with John Colbert than just not being very smart, but he refrained from voicing his opinion.

"What about Ethan?"

"Ethan was . . . closer to Ana than John was. I don't think he'd have any reason to kill her."

"Would he have used a knife?"

"Possibly, but he wouldn't have . . . cut her up like that."

Clint made a note to talk to either the chief, or the coroner as to exactly how Ana Colbert had been killed. He also reminded himself that he wanted to talk to Inspector Chevalier before this day passed. He had the feeling that the man was avoiding him.

"What about Inspector Chevalier, the man who arrested Tarr? Do you know him?"

"Yes."

"Did Ana know him?"

"Yes."

"Well?"

She didn't answer.

"Had she slept with him?"

"I believe so."

"How old is Chevalier?"

"Oh . . . about thirty or so, I guess."

"How well does your husband know him?"

"My husband knows the chief and the inspector very well, and some of the other officers in the police department as well."

"Alicia, I'm going to ask you something about your husband that you may not want to answer. It may make you feel . . . disloyal." It struck him what an odd thing that was to say to a woman about her husband when he had just had a rather energetic sexual encounter with her.

"I couldn't feel disloyal to that bastard!" she spat. "Ask whatever you want."

"A man of his wealth and influence, he must have someone to . . . to do his dirty work for him. Would that be this fella Frank Marlowe you mentioned?"

"Oh, no," she said. "Marlowe is an errand boy, and not much of a man as far as I'm concerned. No, the man who would do his dirty work is Douglas Proffit."

"Proffit?" Clint didn't know the name. "What does he do?"

"Not much," she said. "He dresses well, and speaks well, and uses all the correct utensils at the table, but there's a look in his eyes that frightens me."

"Would the police know about him?"

"I'm sure," she said. "He's known to have killed some men in New Orleans, but always manages to make it appear justified."

"Killed some men? For your husband, you mean?"

"I can't say that for sure," she said, "but Proffit isn't afraid to kill, and he can do it several ways."

"With a knife?" Clint asked.

Alicia looked thoughtful for a moment and then said, "Yes, I believe he has been known to use a knife."

Clint made a mental note to look into the whereabouts of Douglas Proffit at the time Ana Colbert was being killed.

"I have to get back to the house," she said.

It was late, still night, tehnically, although fast approaching early morning hours.

"Won't your husband wonder where you are?"

"I doubt it," she said. "He didn't come home, which means he's probably with . . . with his mistress."

"Louise Killough."

"Yes," she said tightly, "she is the current one. Before her he was sleeping with our black maid, Samantha."

"And she still works for you?"

"I insisted that we keep her," Alicia said. "He used to sneak down to her room and have sex with her in her bed, then come back up to our bed. I could smell her on him."

"Why did you insist on keeping her, then?"

"She was only trying to keep her job," Alicia said. "She wasn't at fault."

"And Louise Killough?"

"That's different," Alicia said, but she did not explain how, and he didn't pursue it.

She approached the bed and leaned over to kiss him.

"Thank you," she said.

"Don't be silly."

"I won't bother you anymore . . . if you don't want me to."

"You didn't bother me, Alicia."

"I mean, if you're involved with Julie—"

"I've known you and Julie the same length of time," he said, "and I don't consider that I'm involved with either of you—not in the usual connotation that the word 'involved' carries. Do you understand?"

"I understand," she said. "I understand perfectly. I have to go. I'll . . . see you . . ."

"We'll see each other."

She walked to the door, put her hand on the doorknob, then turned to face him again.

"You didn't ask me . . ." she said.

"Ask you what?"

"You didn't ask me if I thought Robert killed our daughter."

He frowned.

"It didn't occur to me to ask . . . about a father killing his own daughter."

"No," she said, looking past him at something only she could see, "no, I guess not."

After she left, he thought about it for the first time.

Robert Colbert had Louise Killough's firm ass in his hands and was driving his rigid penis in and out of her as hard and fast as he could. He liked it that way, hard and fast. It had never occurred to him to ask Louise— or any of the other women he'd been with—how *they* wanted it. To Robert Colbert it only mattered what he wanted, and what he liked.

Besides which, Louise didn't seem to be complaining much. She was too busy clinging to him, moaning and crying out in his ear.

Finally, Colbert roared and emptied himself into her and immediately rolled off of her.

"Do you have to go home tonight?" she asked.

Lying on his back staring at the ceiling, regulating his breathing, Colbert said, "What for?"

"If you feel that way," she asked, "why do you stay married to her?"

He turned his face towards her and said, "She's my wife, Louise," with an odd look on his face.

Louise Killough turned her face away and studied the wall on her side of the bed.

Robert Colbert was the oddest Catholic she had ever known. He would have sex with other women, but he would never dream of divorcing his wife, with whom he had *not* had sex in over four years.

She wondered what he told the priest when he went to confession.

"Go to sleep," he told her. "When you wake up, I'll be gone."

He ignored her after that and thought about Douglas

Proffit. He never asked Proffit how he would accomplish the things he was being paid to do, but this time he wondered about it.

He had told Proffit that he wanted Clint Adams out of New Orleans. He did not want the man asking questions about his daughter's death.

He wondered how Proffit intended to accomplish that little task.

TWENTY-ONE

In the morning Clint had breakfast in the hotel dining room and found out that they could do eggs and potatoes pretty well.

After breakfast he walked to the police station. Officer Hautala was once again seated at the desk and Clint asked to see Inspector Chevalier.

"He's not in, sir."

"Where is he?"

"Out."

"You don't know where?"

"No, sir," the officer said. "He's on duty."

"I see. Would Chief Thoreau be able to see me now?"

"I'll ask, sir."

He asked, and Clint was shown into Thoreau's office.

"How are you, Mr. Adams? I've been thinking about you."

"Should I be flattered?"

"Not at all," Thoreau said. "Please, have a seat."

Clint remained standing.

"Chief, could you tell me why I'm having so much difficulty getting to see Inspector Chevalier?"

He expected the chief to make some excuse or other, and was surprised when the man said, "Perhaps he doesn't want to talk to you."

"Now why would that be?"

"I do not know," Thoreau said. "I only suggested it as a possibility. I can't answer any questions for the inspector."

"Does he have an office here?"

"He does."

"So I'll just have to keep looking for him? Trying to catch him in?"

"I suppose so."

"Chief, can you tell me how the girl was killed?"

"The girl?" the chief said. "Ana Colbert?"

"Yes, Ana Colbert."

The chief considered the question, then apparently saw no harm in answering it.

"She was stabbed."

"How many times?"

"That's an odd question."

"Why do you say that?"

"If she was stabbed she was stabbed. Why should it matter how many times?"

"If she was stabbed several times, or more, it might indicate great anger on the part of her killer. Maybe he—or she—had something personal against her."

"Sure he did," the chief said. "She wouldn't go to bed with him."

"You're speaking of Justin Tarr."

"I am."

"How many times was she stabbed? Could you tell me that?"

Thoreau sighed, opened his top drawer and took out a file. He found the page that he wanted, read it, and then closed the file and put it away.

"Forty-one times," he said.

"I'm sorry," Clint said, "did you say forty-one times?"

"I did," the chief said. "You're friend was apparently *very* upset."

"How did he seem in court?"

"Very subdued."

"Like a man who had stabbed a young girl forty-one times?"

"I don't know," the chief said. "I never met a man who would stab a beautiful young woman forty-one times—until now."

Clint moved towards the door.

"Thank you for your time, Chief."

"You're welcome."

"Oh," Clint said at the door, "I understand you spoke with the Colberts, about the attack on me?"

"I did."

The chief did not go on to elaborate.

"Well, I don't want to press charges."

The chief smiled and said, "That's kind of you."

Clint left wondering what would have happened if he had wanted to press charges.

TWENTY-TWO

Douglas Proffit didn't know who Clint Adams was.

Before Proffit made any decision on how he was going to handle this, he wanted to find out who Clint Adams was. Proffit was careful that way. That's why he was still alive, and why some eleven men had lost their lives at his hands. That was eleven men that he had been paid to kill—only three by Robert Colbert, but then Proffit worked for other people too. This did not, however, count the men Proffit had killed on his own, in bars, or in duels. Duels were not tolerated any more in New Orleans, but Proffit had still been able to build a reputation as a peerless duelist. There were ways around everything.

Proffit went to the offices of the *New Orleans Star* and gained access to their morgue files. The *Star* was not a major New Orleans newspaper, but then the word wouldn't get around that Proffit had been there.

The *Star* often picked up stories from other newspapers, and often stories from the West. It was in one such story that Proffit found out who Clint Adams was.

Armed with the name "The Gunsmith," Proffit then went to the library where he was able to read more about the man called Clint Adams.

It was all very interesting reading.

When Proffit left the library he was excited, so excited that he went to the home of a widow named Sally O'Shay and took her to bed. Sally O'Shay was thirty-eight years old, had been widowed some four years, and was enjoying her newfound freedom. Proffit was not the only man she slept with, but he didn't care about that. She was there when he wanted her, which had been an added stipulation when she had hired him to kill her wealthy, octogenarian husband who had seemed bent on living forever. She had paid him a generous fee and made herself available to him when he wanted a bedmate. It saved him the annoyance of trying to find a woman he wanted in the French Quarter or somewhere, one that he could be assured was clean.

In the four years since he had killed her husband, making her a widow, she had never turned him away when he came to her door with a stiff dick.

This was no exception.

"Well," Sally O'Shay said. She was breathing hard, and her opulent breasts were gleaming with perspiration. She had the biggest breasts he had ever seen on a woman, and wondered why they didn't hang to her knees when she was standing up.

The rest of her body matched her breasts. Sally was well-fed, with ample hips and buttocks accentuated by a trim waist that truly gave her the look of an hourglass.

Physically, she wasn't exactly the kind of woman Proffit preferred.

Alicia Colbert was the kind of woman he really preferred, but she was married to the man who paid him very well to take care of his dirty work. Proffit did not shit where he lived, and so he went to Sally O'Shay whenever he had the need to dip his wick, so to speak.

"Well," Sally O'Shay said again, "what got you so worked up?"

"Never mind," he said. He was lying on his back, smoking a long, thin, brown cigar, contemplating the smoke as it rose to the ceiling.

"Not that I'm complaining, mind you," she said. "I haven't had a ride like that in months. A lot of the young men I've been seeing don't really know how to treat a woman like me. Jesus, I've had to *teach* more of them—hell, maybe I'll start looking for older men, you know? With more experience."

"Serves you right for liking the young ones, Sally," Proffit said.

"Yeah, I know, but I get all wet between my legs when I see a twenty year old lad with big shoulders, or a pretty face. I just naturally wonder what he's got between his legs."

"It's not what they've got," Proffit said, "it's how they use it."

"I'm starting to believe *that*."

They lay silent for a few moments, the only sound made by Proffit when he blew the smoke towards the ceiling.

Finally she asked, "So who are you going to kill this time?"

"What?"

"When you come here this worked up I usually check

the newspapers for the next few days, and somebody usually turns up dead—only you've never been this worked up. It must be somebody big, this time."

He turned to look at her and said, "Sally, you're asking too many questions."

"I'm just curious, Proffit—" she started, but he leaned over and pressed the lit end of the cigar to her left breast, just missing the nipple. For a moment she looked shocked, and then she screamed and sat up, slapping her chest.

"Jesus Christ—" she screamed. "That hurt!"

"It was supposed to," he said. He pressed the cigar against her so hard it had gone out, and he dropped it to the floor and stood up, starting to dress.

"How am I going to explain this burn?" she demanded, still rubbing it.

"Tell your next young lover that you like it rough," he said.

"You're a bastard, Proffit!"

"Remember that," he said, "the next time you want to ask so many questions."

"Jesus—" she said again. There was a glass of liquor on the table next to her with some ice cubes in it. She snatched one out and pressed it to the burn.

"Is this gonna scar?" she demanded.

"It may," he said, walking to the door, pulling on his black leather gloves. "If it does let me know, and I'll fix it so the other one matches."

Outside on the street he reminded himself to send her some roses. He'd struck her before, once or twice, but he'd never done anything to scar her. This was the first time, but she *had* been asking too many questions. Maybe this would teach her not to.

Under other circumstances, after she had revealed to him that she was aware of his established pattern—fuck her, then go out and kill someone—he would have killed her. But he knew that if she were ever to turn him in, she'd have to explain how she came to know him.

He just couldn't see her going to the police and saying, "Yes, I met him when I hired him to kill my husband, and he's been fucking me ever since."

Besides, she liked it too much when he did come around. It gave her a break from the young ones she was always bringing home.

Proffit went home to his two rooms in the French Quarter now. He had to assimilate everything he had learned about Clint Adams, and decide the best way to handle the man who was known throughout the West as "The Gunsmith."

This, he thought, would be the biggest challenge of his career.

TWENTY-THREE

Inspector Emil Chevalier sat in the lobby of the Napoleon Hotel, waiting for Clint Adams to arrive.

In truth, Inspector Chevalier had not exactly been avoiding Adams. He had not been going out of his way to meet him, either, but he had decided only fifteen minutes ago that it was time. He didn't want Adams to constantly be talking to the chief about him. This way was better. Talk to the man and get it out of the way.

"Would you like some coffee out here, Inspector?" the desk man asked, solicitously.

"No, thank you," Chevalier said. "I'm fine. Please, just let me wait in silence."

"Yes, sir," the man said, "of course, sir."

The clerk retreated behind the desk but couldn't help watching the inspector the whole time. He knew who Chevalier was waiting to see. Most of the people in

New Orleans knew that Chevalier was a man to be feared.

Maybe the stranger from the West was about to discover the same thing.

When Clint Adams entered the hotel he saw the man sitting in the lobby and knew something was up.

He saw the clerk nod to the seated man, who rose and moved to intercept him. The man was tall, with broad shoulders and a tapered waist, and a suit cut to show these things.

"Mr. Adams?"

"That's right."

"I understand you have been looking for me."

"That depends on who you are."

"My name is Chevalier, Emil Chevalier," the man said, and then with practiced ease added, "Inspector."

Clint studied the man and decided that he liked being who he was. Perhaps he was to be envied for that.

"Yes, indeed," Clint said, "I have been looking forward to meeting you, Inspector. Is there somewhere we can talk?"

"In the dining room?" Chevalier said. He saw the look on Clint's face and added, "Their French food is atrocious, but they make very good Cajun dishes. Let me buy you some crawfish."

"All right," Clint said.

"Excellent," Chevalier said, and smiled, showing very white teeth.

Clint felt like he was looking at the smile of a mountain lion just before he devoured his prey.

Before returning to his hotel and finding the inspector there waiting for him, Clint had gone once again to

Louise Killough's hat shop. As he entered, the woman behind the counter saw him and dropped the hat she was showing to an older woman.

"I—I'm sorry," she said to the woman.

Clint moved aside and waited for her to finish with her customer.

As the older woman left, Clint approached the counter.

"What do you want?" Louise Killough demanded. "I don't have to talk to you."

"That's true, Louise, you don't," Clint said, "but I'm going to hope that you will, anyway."

"I won't."

"You know, you can go to jail for perjury. Do you know what perjury is?"

"Please," Louise said, closing her eyes as if she hoped he would be gone when she opened them again, "leave me alone."

"Lying on the stand, under oath, that's perjury, and it's against the law. You can go to jail for that."

"I didn't . . ."

"You didn't what?"

"I didn't lie."

"I think you did."

They stared at each other for a few moments, and then Louise said, "I'm going to go for the police."

"Good," he said, "ask them to send Inspector Chevalier. He arrested Justin Tarr, and I'd like to talk to him, as well."

"I—I have to close up."

"That's all right," he said, "I'm leaving. Tell Colbert I'm still waiting to talk to him."

"I—I—I don't—" she stammered.

"I'm leaving now," he said, "but we'll talk again—real soon."

He left her and knew she'd close up after him. She was too shaken up to work. Maybe she'd go and talk to Colbert. Maybe this time he'd be angry enough to come after him.

And maybe he'd just send someone to do the job for him.

Like a man called Proffit.

Clint still knew nothing about the man called Douglas Proffit. He had meant to ask the chief about him, but in the end had decided not to. The chief was not being all that cooperative, except when it came to facts that were readily available to him. Still, he had refused to give him Louise Killough's name as the star witness, even though he knew Clint would find out, anyway.

That might have been in deference to Robert Colbert, however. Thoreau could always tell Colbert that Clint had not gotten her name from him, no sir.

Following Inspector Chevalier into the hotel dining room, Clint was sure that the inspector would be able to tell him all he needed to know about Douglas Proffit.

TWENTY-FOUR

"How is it?" Chevalier asked.

Clint looked up from his plate of crawfish and said, "It's excellent."

"For the remainder of your stay here," Chevalier said, "make sure you order from their Cajun menu. Their chef is Cajun, and doesn't know the first thing about real French cooking."

"I'll remember," Clint said. "Thank you."

"Now," Chevalier said, sitting back in his chair, "what was it you wanted to see me about?"

"Justin Tarr."

"Ah," the inspector said, "a terrible thing. I understand he's really quite a gentle man. You have to watch out for the gentle ones. When they snap, they go completely crazy."

"Is that what you think happened?"

"I feel sure of it."

"I am not so sure."

"Indeed? Who do you think killed poor Ana Colbert?"

"I don't know," Clint said, "but I'm looking into it."

"Ah, then you're a detective?" Chevalier said. "Perhaps a Pinkerton?"

"No, I'm not a detective," Clint said, "I'm just a friend of his."

"I see. Well, as the arresting officer I feel sure I arrested the right man, Mr. Adams. He was identified by an eyewitness—"

"An eyewitness to what?"

"I beg your pardon?"

"What exactly did Louise Killough see?"

"Oh, well, she saw him running from the scene of the murder with blood on his hands. Pretty damning, wouldn't you say?"

"She didn't see him kill her, then?"

"Oh, no."

"And yet her testimony convicted him."

"Well," the inspector said, "no one *else* was seen leaving the scene. Logically, we feel he had exclusive opportunity."

That sounded like a legal term to Clint, and probably meant exactly what it sounded like it meant.

"Do you have concrete proof that he ever knew her?"

"Oh, yes."

"What's that?"

"It's all a matter of record, Mr. Adams," Chevalier said. "They were seen dining together at a small café in the French Quarter."

"And who saw them?"

"Why, Louise Killough."

"She just happened to be in that café, and near the

scene of the murder as well? Isn't that a little coinciden-tal?"

"Isn't that what catches murderers, Mr. Adams? Co-incidence? Carelessness? If you *were* a detective you would know this."

"Well, I hope you won't mind if I operate under the assumption that you've got the wrong man."

"Go right ahead," Chevalier said. "In a matter of days it won't matter much, anyway."

Silently, Clint agreed.

Clint abstained from dessert and settled for coffee. The inspector asked for a simple piece of apple pie to go with his coffee.

"Tell me, Inspector, do you know a man named Douglas Proffit?"

"Very well," Chevalier said. "Where did you run across him?"

"I haven't, yet," Clint said, "just his name. When you say you know him very well, does that mean that you are friends?"

"Not at all," Chevalier said. "The man is a killer, but I have not been able to pin him down. His murders are always cloaked in . . . ah, legitimacy, shall we say? He always has the right answers to all the questions."

"I see."

"Do you plan on talking to him?"

"If I can locate him. Will that be easier than locating you was?"

Chevalier laughed.

"He lives in the French Quarter," the inspector said. "If you like, I will take you right to his home and you can talk to him."

Clint considered that, then decided that he did not want the inspector present when he spoke to Proffit.

"Maybe you could just give me directions," he said.

"As you wish," Chevalier said, and did so.

They left the dining room together and stopped in the lobby.

"I'll be going up to my room to try to digest some of this excellent crawfish you've introduced me to," Clint said.

"And I will be returning to my duties. Please, if you need my assistance, don't hesitate to call on me."

"If I can find you."

The inspector laughed and said, "Please, believe me when I say that I have not been avoiding you. I will tell the officers at the station where I am at all times, so that you can find me if you need me. I'd like you to be convinced that I arrested the right man."

"Is that the only reason you're making yourself so helpful?" Clint asked.

"No," Chevalier said, frankly. "No, the real reason is, I would hate to think that I arrested and caused the execution of the wrong man."

As the inspector left, Clint wasn't sure whether he believed him or not. Their conversation had been so civilized, and yet he had the distinct impression that the inspector was not, deep down, a very civilized man.

TWENTY-FIVE

Proffit sat in the café, alone at his table, waiting. The only time he ever came here was when he had to meet with his brother. Of course, no one knew that they were brothers. They had come to New Orleans separately, his brother first, and he sometime later, after his brother had established himself here.

As brothers they were not so close. It was only lately, when their business had brought them together, that they had started seeing each other.

He was thinking about that—and their father—when he saw his brother enter the café. He didn't rise, but signaled the waiter to bring another glass of brandy.

"Brandy," his brother said, sitting. "Still drinking that shit."

"It's refined," Proffit said.

"Refined," his brother said, picking up the glass. "What would Poppa say if he could see his two 'refined' sons? Our poppa, the dirt farmer who thought 'refined' was something you did to dirt."

"Never mind Poppa," Proffit said.

"You ever think about him?" his brother asked.

"No," Proffit lied.

"Me neither."

"Proffit" was not Douglas Proffit's real name. It was a name he took when he came to New Orleans, because it was the only thing that interested him, making a profit in life.

He'd spent many years in the East, in New York and Pennsylvania, a little time in Washington, D.C. It was there he learned how to kill, and when he had mastered his new profession, he had come to New Orleans to ply it.

"What was it you had to see me about?" Proffit asked.

"There's a man looking for you."

"So? A lot of men have come looking for me, and have been sorry they ever found me. What's this one's name?"

"Adams," his brother said, "Clint Adams."

Proffit's eyes and face betrayed nothing, it was only inside that he jerked at the sound of the name.

"I see. What does he want?"

"I don't know," his brother replied. "I only know that he's investigating the death of Ana Colbert."

"I had no hand in that."

"If you say so," the other man said, "I'm just warning you."

"Thanks for the warning. Anything else?"

"No," his brother said, "no new business."

"Then don't contact me again until you *do* have some new business."

His brother stared at him, then stood up.

"I don't know much about Adams, but he didn't strike me as a fool, and he looks and sounds competent."

"I'll let you know how competent he is," Proffit promised.

"Yeah," his brother said.

They stared at each other for a few moments, brothers who had not felt like brothers in many years, and then he turned and left.

Proffit signaled the waiter to bring him a beer and wondered why Clint Adams was looking for him.

TWENTY-SIX

Robert Colbert was annoyed.

He had told Louise Killough not to come to his office, ever, and yet here she was, sitting across from his desk, nervously nibbling at her lower lip.

It might be time, he thought, for a new *friend*.

"Louise, I told you this is being taken care of."

"But he came to the store again!" she said.

Colbert could only hope that people would assume that she was there applying for a loan, or something. For all his wealth and business smarts, when it came to his *affairs* he was remarkably naive. He actually thought that no one knew about them—except perhaps, Alicia.

"Just lie to him," he said.

"I have."

"Then you have nothing to fear."

"But he's going to come back!"

"Louise, for God's sake."

The more she nibbled on her lower lip the more he wanted her. He had an erection that was threatening to burst from his pants. He felt like throwing her up on the desk, spread-eagling her and taking her right there.

One more time, he thought, before he dropped her and moved on to someone else. He had no one in mind at the moment, but there was always Samantha. He smiled fondly at the memory of the first time he had gone to her room. He had entered the room without knocking, and she had looked up at him in surprise.

"Mistuh Colbert," she said.

She had been about to get into bed and was wearing a floor-length, flannel nightgown.

"Do you like working here, Samantha?" he'd asked her. She'd only been there a month.

"Yessuh."

"You wouldn't want to lose your job, would you?" he asked, moving closer to her.

She straightened up, standing up against her bed. She was small, about five one, and he had noticed what pert breasts she had, how slim her waist was. She had these big, soft-looking lips that he'd often fantasized about, seeing them wrapped around his rigid cock.

"Well then," he said to her, "we should get to know each other a little better, shouldn't we?"

Her eyes were wide as she stared at him, but he knew that she knew what he meant.

"Yessuh."

She didn't move when he raised her nightgown, unveiling her little by little. Below the waist she was a bit chunky, like most black women he'd ever seen. Heavy thighs, high, firm ass. The hair between her legs was the blackest he had ever seen, and it crawled up her belly almost to her navel. When he removed the nightgown completely, he saw her small but firm breasts with their chocolate brown nipples.

He opened his own dressing gown then, revealing his nakedness to her, his readiness. He had put his hand behind her head and guided her face down to his crotch. She had parted her lips and he slid right into her mouth, those fleshy lips wrapped around him as they had in his fantasies . . .

"Robert, are you listening to me?" Louise Killough demanded shrilly, bringing him from his reverie. He detested shrill women, and now his lust had been transferred from her to Samantha, sweet little Samantha, working right there in his own home . . .

"I hear you, Louise," he said, patiently. "All I can tell you is go back to your shop and wait. This will all be over soon. When that . . . that gambler hangs, Adams will have no reason to stay—unless he leaves even before then, as I suspect he will."

"Robert—"

"For Godssake, Louise, go home!"

"Will you come later?"

Colbert thought about Samantha's lips and said vaguely, "Maybe . . ."

As Louise left he shifted in his chair to try and take the pressure off his erection. The last thing he wanted to do was soil his pants. He couldn't leave now to go home, he had too much to do.

Suddenly he remembered the young woman he'd hired last month as a teller. She was about twenty, slender, with blonde hair and green eyes and full lips— not as full as Samantha's, but then there was that blonde hair, as fair as Samantha's was black.

He went to the door of his office and said, "Frank," to Frank Marlowe, his assistant.

"Yes, sir?"

"What's the name of that new teller?

"Jim Sands?"

"No, damn it, the girl."

"Oh, Angela Tompkins."

"That's the one," Colbert said. "Send her in, will you?"

"Is something wrong?"

"There will be if you don't send her in!" Colbert snapped.

"Yes, sir."

Colbert walked back to his desk and seated himself behind it. It never occurred to him that she might refuse. After all, she worked for him and he paid her well.

Besides, this was just a stopgap until he got home tonight, where Samantha would be waiting . . .

"Mr. Colbert?"

He looked up at the door and there she was, a sweet young thing with an angelic face that he wanted to stick his dick into.

"Come in, my dear . . ."

It was over, of that Louise Killough was sure.

As she went back to her shop she knew that Robert Colbert was about to leave her, and this angered her. She had perjured herself for him, lied so that a man would be convicted, possibly for something he had not done. Colbert was sure that the man had killed his daughter, but Louise knew that it could have been any number of men in New Orleans. Colbert was blind when it came to Ana, but Louise knew her for the slut she really was.

Granted, Colbert had set her up in her business. She

was not coming out of the relationship—if it could be called that—empty-handed, but she was also being badgered by Clint Adams, and there was the chance that she could go to jail, for Chrissake!

If Colbert thought he was going to get rid of her that easily, he was sadly mistaken.

TWENTY-SEVEN

Clint hadn't seen Julie all day, and now he wondered if he wanted to. After spending part of last night with her aunt—after telling her that he was too tired to spend it with her—he didn't like the idea of her finding out. True, there was almost nothing between them, but still he felt funny about it, almost as if he had slept with a girlfriend's mother, or something.

Only, in bed, Alicia Colbert was like no one's mother.

He wondered now if he had done the right thing by sleeping with her. She was, after all, still recovering from the death—no, the *murder* of her daughter. Maybe going to bed with him was just a . . . a by-product of the pressure she must be feeling. Lord knew she had enough to feel pressure about. A murdered daughter, a cheating husband, a moron son, and Ethan—whatever Ethan's problem was.

Back to Julie.

What would he say to Julie when he saw her?

Hi, I had sex with your aunt last night?

Hi, guess who came to my room last night?

Guess what?

Shit.

"I thought we wasn't supposed to do nothing to him no more," John Colbert said.

"John," Ethan said, "for the millionth time, since we've been kids I've been telling you to let me do the thinking, okay?"

"I know, but Poppa said—"

"He's hired Proffit to take care of this for him, John," Ethan said, slowly. "Does that sound like he wants nothing done?"

"No, I mean he don't want *us* doing nothing to Adams . . ." John said.

"John, Adams broke your wrist. Are you gonna let him get away with that?"

John frowned mightily and said, "I thought you broke my wrist."

"I did . . . but it was his fault—and he punched me in the nose."

"Does it still hurt?"

"Of course it still hurts."

"But the doctor said it wasn't broken—"

"Well, it hurts anyway, all right?"

It was getting dark and the Colbert boys were standing in a doorway across the street from the Napoleon Hotel.

"Look there . . ." Ethan said, suddenly.

John looked and saw Julie Graft walking toward the hotel.

"That's Cousin Julie," John said.

"Wouldn't I like to get to know Cousin Julie better," Ethan said, feeling a thickening in his crotch.

"Maybe we can, Ethan," John said, "if Poppa lets her move in—"

"He doesn't want her to move into our house," Ethan said, "not that I'd mind sharing a bathtub with her."

"That wouldn't be right, would it, Ethan?" John asked. "I mean, she's family."

Ethan looked at John.

"Is this the guy who was caught naked with little Ana when she was just thirteen? Naughty, naughty, John, letting your own sister suck on your—"

"It was her idea!" John said. "She said it was all right because we were brother and sister!"

"And you believed her."

"I didn't think she'd lie to me," John said, sullenly.

"John, everybody in this world will lie to you," Ethan said.

"Even you, Ethan?"

"I'm the only one who *wouldn't* lie to you, brother," Ethan said. "You believe that, don't you?"

"Sure I do, Ethan," John said. "Sure I do."

"Moron," Ethan said, and caught a final glimpse of "Cousin Julie" before she entered the hotel.

Julie Graft was confused.

Last night, after she had gone to her room, she'd decided to go to Clint's room and see if he would let her spend the night with him. Just to sleep, she was going to tell him, nothing else. When she got to his room she heard voices from inside.

His voice.

And a woman's voice.

Since her room was just down the hall from his she decided—out of curiousity, of course—to see who the woman was. She stood at her door, waiting for the woman to come out.

She stood there for three hours and then got the shock of her life when her Aunt Alicia came out.

Aunt Alicia, of all people!

There couldn't be any doubt of what they were doing in there for three hours, and after Clint had said all he wanted to do was sleep.

At first she was angry. Clint had lied to her. After twenty minutes of anger, though, she had calmed down. After all, they weren't married, they weren't even engaged, and maybe he had known Alicia before he knew *her*.

Julie admitted that even at her age—probably her late forties—Aunt Alicia was a beautiful woman, and Clint *was* closer to Aunt Alicia's age than he was to her own twenty-seven.

Did she have any right at all to feel anger, or hurt? Or anything?

What would she say to Clint when she saw him?

I came to your room last night and guess what I heard?

I watched your room last night and guess who I saw leaving?

Was Aunt Alicia as good as I was—or better?

Guess what?

Aunt Alicia!

Hell.

Clint was coming down the stairs just as Julie entered the hotel.

Kismet.

Fate.

Whatever you called it, it was unavoidable.

They met face to face in the center of the lobby.

"Uh—" he said.

"Um—" she said.

They stood like that for a while and then he said, "Let's get some dinner and talk."

"Okay," she replied, "let's."

TWENTY-EIGHT

Over dinner—ordered off the Cajun menu—Clint told Julie what had happened last night.

After he finished, Julie told Clint what she had done last night.

"Well," he said when she was finished, "have you ever run into a more honest pair than us?"

"No, I don't think so," she said.

"Your aunt likes you," he said.

Did she tell you that before or after—she started to think, but then stopped herself.

"Clint—"

"I know," he said. "I don't blame you."

"For what?"

"For not wanting to see me again."

"Would that bother you?" she asked.

"Yes," he said. "I thought we were on our way to becoming friends."

"And what about you and Aunt Alicia?"

"That's a tough one," he said. "I don't know what we are—I don't think we're friends."

"Lovers?"

"As much as you and I are," he said, "maybe less."

"Why less?"

He stared at her.

Julie continued, "Oh, you've only slept with her once, is that it?"

He didn't answer.

"Did you sleep with her only to get information?" she asked suddenly.

"What would you want to hear me say to that?" he asked.

"The truth."

"No," he said, "I did it because . . . I was attracted to her, and because of the . . . the situation."

"The situation?"

"Sort of like the first night with us," he said. "It was . . . unexpected, it was . . . exciting."

"With both of us?"

"Yes."

"Well . . ." she said.

The silence hung between them for a while and then she said, "I did some filing for Carl today. I think he'll be surprised when he gets back."

"I hope I'm surprised when he gets back," Clint said.

"What do you mean?"

"If he returns with a pardon I'll be pleasantly surprised."

"You don't think he will?"

"A man like your uncle, his influence spreads a long way. I never knew a rich man who didn't have connections in the state capital."

"Then why did you send Carl?"

"It was a move that had to be made," he said.

"Like last night with my aunt?"

"Julie—"

"I'm sorry," she said, raising her hands, "I shouldn't have said that. I guess this . . . bothers me more than it should, more than I have a right to be bothered. I mean, it's not like we're engaged, or anything."

"I understand."

"Do you?"

"I think I do."

"I'll need some time."

"I don't have time, Julie," he said. "Whether or not I get Justin off, I'll be leaving New Orleans soon."

"Oh."

"I hope we can stay friends."

She stared at him and then a look came over her face, one like relief.

"I guess that would be the easiest thing, wouldn't it?" she asked. "To just be friends?"

"I guess so."

"All right, then," she said, "friends."

She extended her hand across the table and he took it and shook it.

"What's your next move?"

"I have to find a man named Proffit."

"Who is he?"

"Apparently, he's the man Colbert calls when he needs someone . . . ah, killed."

"Oh."

"I'm sorry, Julie, I know he's your uncle—"

"You don't think he had his own daughter killed, do you? He couldn't be that much of a monster."

"Maybe not, but I'm just trying to cover every

move," he said. "I've talked to your uncle's mistress twice, I've talked to Inspector Chevalier and the chief—"

"You found the inspector?" she asked, surprised.

"He found me," he said, and told her about the lunch they had.

"God, he sounds smooth," she said.

"Too smooth. Anyway, who's left to talk to?"

She thought a moment and then said, "The boys?"

"The boys?"

"John and Ethan."

"Why them?"

She shrugged and said, "You said you had to cover every move. That would seem a logical one."

Now he took a moment and then said, "You know, you're right. I guess I'll talk to them tomorrow."

"Together, or separately?"

"That's a good point, too," he said. "Maybe I'll get more out of John without Ethan around."

"How will you separate them?"

"Are they always together?"

"As far as I know."

"Well," he said, "maybe you can help me with that . . ."

TWENTY-NINE

"Should we go in and get him?" John asked.

"Into the hotel?" Ethan said. "That's real good, John. Nobody would recognize us."

"We could go in the back."

Ethan stared at John, surprised at what had sounded like a fairly good idea. Still . . .

"There'd still be a chance that someone would see us," he said to his younger brother. "No, we've got to wait for him to come out."

"What if he don't?"

"It's early," Ethan said. "He'll come out, looking for a card game, or a woman—"

"Julie's in there."

"You think he and Julie are—naw!" Ethan said. "I'll bet they don't even know each other. No, he'll come out, all right, and when he does we'll be waiting for him. How's your arm?"

"It hurts."

"I know that. What I want to know is, am I going to have to do all the work?"

"No," John said, "I can handle him."

"Good."

"Ethan?"

"Yeah?"

"Just don't hit me with nothin' this time, okay?"

"John," Ethan said wearily, "it was a goddamned accident—"

"I know," John said, "I don't blame you—"

"Then shut up about it, okay?"

"Okay, Ethan," John said in his wounded tone.

Ethan hated John's wounded tone. As big as his brother was, his wounded tone always made him seem like a dog who had just been kicked.

"We're doing what's right, John," Ethan said, touching his brother's shoulder affectionately. "I promise you."

"All right, Ethan."

The relationship between the brothers was an odd one. In truth, John was the only person Ethan had any feelings for, any *love* for. He hated his mother, because he knew she hated them; he respected his father, but he knew that his father had only loved Ana.

John didn't know what to think, he was confused by all of them except Ethan. Ethan took care of him— breaking his wrist *had* been an accident—and looked out for him, and he looked out for Ethan. John didn't know what love was, but he guessed that if he loved anyone it was Ethan.

All those years ago, when thirteen-year-old Ana had tricked the sixteen-year-old John into taking off all his clothes and getting into his bed with her, he had felt like maybe she loved him. When she had let him touch her breasts—big breasts, with big, pretty pink nipples, even though she was only thirteen—he had thought it meant she loved him. And when she had taken his huge cock into her mouth he had thought it meant she loved him.

It was Ethan who told him that she was laughing at him the whole time, and when Momma had caught them it was him she had yelled at, like it was his fault.

Later Ethan told John that, back then, even Momma didn't know what Ana was really like.

Now they both knew what she was like.

"Did she ever do that to you, Ethan?" John had asked only recently, after Ana's death.

"She tried, John," Ethan said, "but I showed her who was in charge."

"How?"

"She was sixteen then. Remember how damned pretty she was at sixteen?"

"I remember."

"Well, I plowed her like a field," Ethan said. "I rammed it into her until she begged me for more. Shit, after that one time she's always wanted it again, but I never gave it to her."

"Golly," John said.

It never occurred to him that maybe Ethan was lying.

"Is that what you want to do to Julie, Ethan?"

"What?"

"You know, plow her like a field, ram it into her . . . like that?"

"Yeah," Ethan said, "cousin or no cousin, I'd like that."

"Me, too," John said, "me, too, I'd like that."

"Well then, you can have her, John," Ethan said, "after I finish with her, you can have her."

"Really?"

"Really."

"Gee, thanks, Ethan."

"Let's keep quiet now, John," Ethan said. "Keep quiet and keep an eye on that door, okay?"

"Whatever you say, Ethan."

Ethan looked at his bigger, younger brother and thought with affection, what a dope.

Still, ramming Julie wasn't a bad idea. He knew that his brother was hung like a damned horse, and he was no slouch himself.

He wondered if she'd like it, maybe take them both at the same time?

If it ran in the blood—if she was anything like that whore Ana—she would.

"What are you going to do now?" Julie asked as they left the dining room and entered the lobby.

"I'm going to the French Quarter to find Proffit," Clint said.

"Is that wise?" she asked. "I mean, at night? In his backyard?"

"I'll be in his backyard, day or night, Julie," Clint said, "and I can't waste time waiting until morning."

"Can I come with you?"

He gave her a look that said she was crazy and said, "No."

"He sounds like someone you might need help against," she said.

"I appreciate the offer, I really do," Clint said, "but I'll do better if I don't have you along to worry about. Understand?"

"Sure, I understand."

"I really do appreciate the offer, though," he said.

She shrugged and said, "What are friends for?"

"There he is," Ethan said.

Clint Adams appeared in the doorway of the hotel and then, to his surprise, Julie Graft appeared next to him. They were talking like they knew each other.

"He does know Julie," John said.

"I can see that."

They watched Julie put her hand on Clint Adams's arm in a familiar way.

"Now we really have to teach him a lesson," Ethan said.

"What do you mean?" John asked.

"She's family, isn't she?" Ethan said. "Adams has to be taught that he can't fool with our family—not with *any* member of our family. Right, brother?"

All pumped up by Ethan's resolve, John nodded, stuck out his jaw and said, "Right!"

Julie touched Clint's arm and said, "Be careful."

"I will."

"Don't get hurt."

"I won't."

She hesitated a moment then said, "I don't have that many friends in New Orleans that I can afford to lose one, you know?"

"I know," he said, "I'll be careful, I promise. Why don't you get some rest."

"I think I will," she said. "I'm also going to rethink my plans. Maybe it's time for me to leave New Orleans and get on with my life."

"Put off making that decision for a couple of days, all right?"

"Why?"

"Same reason," he said. "I don't have that many friends in New Orleans that I can afford to lose one. Deal?"

She grinned and said, "Deal."

He took her hand, squeezed it, and then left the doorway.

As he walked away from the hotel he saw the two figures move out of a doorway across the street and follow him, one big, one smaller.

It didn't take a genius to figure out that the Colbert boys were on the move again.

THIRTY

The French Quarter was well lit and packed with people. This part of New Orleans was like an all-night party. Clint knew that the Colbert boys were having trouble keeping him in sight with all of the people who were on the streets, and he knew he could lose them easily if he wanted to.

He didn't want to.

It was better to know where they were rather than have to worry about where they might pop up.

Clint followed the directions given him by Inspector Chevalier, wondering all the while why the policeman had been so helpful. Also, how did he know exactly where to find a man he'd been trying to put in jail for ... well, for how long? Unless Proffit was so confident that the law couldn't touch him that he didn't bother keeping his whereabouts a secret.

Whatever the case, Chevalier had told Clint where

Proffit lived, and what saloon he could be found drinking, or gambling in. Clint decided to try the saloon first. It was late enough that Proffit would have had dinner already, but too early for a man like Proffit to turn in.

The saloon was one of the livelier places on the street, with loud music coming from within and attractive whores standing outside. If Clint was the kind of man who spent his money on whores, he would have been sorely tempted.

"Sorry, honey," he told one pretty one in particular, "I have business inside."

"Well," she said, taking a deep breath so that her full, young breasts swelled, "I can do my business inside, too, mister."

"Maybe another time."

"Sometime soon, mister?"

"Sure," he lied, "sometime soon."

She moved from him to the next likely candidate and he was sure that he'd been forgotten already.

As he entered the saloon he looked across the street and saw that the Colbert brothers had been approached by two whores and were desperately trying to get rid of them.

He laughed and went inside.

Proffit had been described to him by Chevalier as a tall man who always wore black, even down to black leather gloves. He was a spare man with a mustache, and a killer's eyes. That was what Chevalier had said, "A killer's eyes."

Of course, Clint knew exactly what he meant.

With that description, Clint was able to spot him immediately.

• • •

Proffit saw the Gunsmith as soon as he entered the place.

He knew the man's description from his research. This legend of the West was not particularly impressive looking from a distance, but as the man approached the poker table Proffit was able to see his eyes.

His eyes told everything.

Proffit continued to play the hand he was holding while keeping track of the Gunsmith. He had three of a kind, queens, and felt that he was holding the winning hand.

"Raise two hundred," he said to the man who had bet a hundred dollars.

The other players—four of them—dropped out, leaving only Proffit and the opener. From the corner of his eye Proffit could see Adams watching the proceedings closely.

"Raise, huh?" the other man said.

"That's right," Proffit said.

"You must have a pretty good hand."

"Are you going to talk, or play?" Proffit asked.

The man studied Proffit's face for a few moments, and then said, "Neither. I fold." He threw his cards down and vacated his chair.

Proffit laid his cards down and raked in his winnings.

From everything he had learned about Clint Adams he was sure the man would take the empty seat.

Clint had watched as the man folded and left his chair, and then moved instinctively toward the table.

"Anyone mind if I sit in?" he asked.

There was a general shaking of heads and one man said, "Always glad to have new money."

Proffit looked up, locked eyes with Clint Adams and added, "And new blood."

THIRTY-ONE

Clint looked across at Proffit. The man did not nod, nor did he look away.

"My deal," the man in black said, and dealt out the beginning of a five-card-stud hand, one card down, one card up.

Clint's down card was a king of hearts. His up card was also a king, this one in spades.

The man to his right, showing an ace, opened for fifty dollars.

"Call," Clint said.

Everyone called, including Proffit, who was sitting with a queen showing.

"Coming out," Proffit said, and dealt the second face-up card, the third card over all.

He dropped a ten of spades on Clint's king of spades.

The man with the ace drew a five, but was still high on the table as no one had paired up.

"Bet fifty," he said.

"Raise fifty," Clint said. It was not so large a raise that he would knock anyone out.

Everyone called, including Proffit, again.

Proffit dealt out the fourth card. Nobody improved noticeably as Clint drew another spade card, this one an eight.

"Ace is still high," Proffit said. He had a queen of diamonds, a nine of diamonds and a deuce of diamonds. In Clint's book a three-card flush was the same as nothing.

The ace holder said, "Check to the raiser."

"A hundred," Clint said. In light of what was showing his kings were pretty solid, but he still underplayed his bet.

The man to his left folded, the next man called, and the man to Proffit's right folded.

Proffit studied Clint's cards for a few moments, then said, "Raise a hundred."

The opener, the man with the ace, tossed in the two hundred dollars.

Clint hesitated a moment, then said, "Call," and threw in a hundred.

The other player dropped out, and it was just the three of them.

"Last card," Proffit said, and dealt it out.

The man with the ace got another one and was noticeably pleased.

Clint got a king, giving him a pair on the table.

Proffit drew another diamond, giving him a four card flush.

"Aces," he said.

"A hundred," the man said, happily.

Clint had seen one other ace on the table, and didn't

figure the man for the case ace in the hole.

"Raise two hundred," he said.

"Two . . ." the man with the aces said, but fell silent.

Proffit didn't hesitate.

"Call, and raise two hundred."

Clint knew that a king had been folded by the man on his left. Proffit would have to wonder if *he* had the case king in the hole. Clint felt from the third player's reaction that all he had were the aces showing, and sure enough the man folded.

Now he stared at Proffit and said, "Call."

The man could have had a flush, all right, but when Proffit turned over his hole card it was the queen of spades.

"Jesus," the man who had folded the aces said, "I had you beat!"

Proffit gave him a baleful look and the man fell silent and stared at Clint's hole card.

Clint turned it over and showed that he had three kings. He could hear the third man's sigh of relief that he had not folded the winning hand after all.

Proffit's face showed nothing as Clint raked in his winnings.

The man who had folded the aces picked up the cards, began to shuffle them prior to dealing and said, "Draw poker, gents."

THIRTY-TWO

Clint and Proffit played poker together for the next three hours, and while taking everyone else's money, neither could get the upper hand on the other.

Respect hung in the air between them.

"You gents want a drink on the house?" the bartender said, coming up to the table.

The other players in the game all said they would.

"I wasn't talking to you mugs," the bartender said. "Mr. Proffit?"

"Sure, Leo," Proffit said. "A brandy, the best you've got."

"And you, sir?"

Before Clint could ask, Proffit said, "Bring Mr. Adams the same."

The bartender raised his eyebrows to Clint and said, "That okay with you?"

"Fine."

The bartender went back to the bar to pour the two brandies.

One of the other players said, "That's all for me," and the other three followed his lead.

That left Clint and Proffit.

"Well, Mr. Adams?" Proffit said. "Would you care to continue?"

"Two handed?" Clint said. "With the way we've been playing we could go on all night and still be where we are now."

"True," Proffit said, "we are rather evenly matched."

"It would seem so."

"Why don't we see whose luck is best, though."

"What do you suggest?" Clint asked.

"One freeze-out hand, five cards, dealt face up."

"For what stakes?"

As his answer Proffit pushed everything he had into the center of the table.

Clint was ahead almost three thousand dollars, and figured that Proffit was up about the same. It wasn't the biggest pot he had ever played for, but it seemed to him that this last hand was going to set the tone for whatever would happen thereafter.

He pushed his money into the center of the table.

"Who deals?" he asked.

At that point the bartender appeared with their brandies and placed each glass by the man's elbow.

"What about the bartender?"

"Leo?"

"Yes, sir?" Leo said to Clint.

"Are you a friend of Mr. Proffit's?"

Leo looked at Proffit, who was still looking at Clint, and then said, "I don't believe so, sir. He comes in here a lot, but that don't make us friends."

"Are you afraid of him?"

Again Leo looked at Proffit.

"Yes, sir," he replied.

"Would you deal this hand honestly?"

"If I didn't, Mr. Adams," Leo the bartender said, "I believe Mr. Proffit would kill me."

Clint studied the man for a moment, and then said, "Would you deal the hand, Leo?"

"Be happy to."

Leo took a vacated seat, picked up the cards and shuffled them. People in the saloon crowded around the table to watch.

"Would either of you gentlemen like the room cleared?" Leo asked.

"No," Proffit said.

"Deal," Clint said.

Leo dealt the first card.

A nine of hearts for Clint.

A nine of clubs for Proffit.

He dealt the second card.

A king of spades for Clint.

A king of diamonds for Proffit.

A murmur began to build in the crowd.

Clint looked at Proffit and saw that the man had taken his eyes from him and was looking at the cards. Clint decided to turn his full attention to the cards as well.

Something was happening here.

Leo dealt the third card.

An ace of hearts for Clint.

An ace of diamonds for Proffit.

When Leo dealt the fourth card his hand was noticeably shaking.

The crowd leaned closer to watch the fourth card fall.

A two of spades for Clint.

A seven of hearts for Proffit.

The crowd seemed to relax a bit, and Leo's hand stopped shaking. Proffit and Clint kept looking at the cards.

Clint had an ace-high hand, followed by a king, a nine and a deuce.

Proffit had ace high, with a king, a nine and a seven.

He had the high hand, so far.

The hand hinged on this last card.

Leo dealt it.

Clint got a seven of clubs.

A deuce of clubs fell in front of Proffit.

There was a gasp from the crowd.

Leo dropped the deck and stared at the hands.

Proffit looked at Clint, who looked back, and then Proffit stood up, still looking at the cards.

The odds against this ever happening were off the board!

Except for the suits, they had drawn the exact same hand!

THIRTY-THREE

Douglas Proffit had one secret in life. It was such a
secret that he never even thought about it, let alone had
he ever told anyone about it.

He was superstitious.

To his superstitious sensibilities, he and Clint Adams
having drawn *exactly the same hands* did not bode well
for the job he was supposed to do.

In Proffit's gambler-killer, superstitious mind, killing
Clint Adams after this might also result in his own
death.

He couldn't have explained that to anyone if he tried,
and he certainly wasn't going to be able to explain it to
Robert Colbert.

Despite the fact that he would not collect a huge fee
from Colbert if Clint Adams remained alive, Douglas
Proffit had one aim tonight: get Clint Adams back to his
hotel alive.

For a fleeting moment Clint thought that Proffit was going to flee from the saloon on the dead run. He could see in the man's eyes that the duplicate hands had affected him greatly.

It wasn't doing a hell of a lot for Clint Adams, either.

Clint was not a superstitious man, but in all his years of playing poker he had never seen two identical hands in one game—and certainly not in a two-handed game of freeze out!

He noticed the glass of brandy at his elbow then, picked it up and drank it.

Proffit picked up his own glass and did the same.

"Sh—should we deal again?" Leo asked, finally finding his voice.

Proffit and Clint exchanged glances.

"No," Proffit said.

"No," Clint agreed.

"Then . . . do you each take back your money?"

Proffit stared at the pot.

"All I want is what I came with," he said. He leaned over and counted out about four hundred dollars.

Clint decided he would do the same and took out only the money he'd invested in that first hand.

"What do I do with the rest of this?" Leo asked.

"I don't care," Proffit said.

Clint said, "Give it to the whores on the street and tell them to take the rest of the night off."

"Wh—what?" Leo said.

"You heard him," Proffit said, looking directly at Leo. "And make damned sure they get it, Leo."

"Sure, Mr. Proffit, sure," Leo said, "they'll get it."

"Have you had enough of this place?" Proffit asked Clint.

"Yes."

Both men walked to the exit and stepped outside.

"I've never seen anything like that before," Clint said.

"Nor have I," Proffit said.

"What do we do now, Proffit?" Clint asked.

"I suspect you came looking for me for a reason," Proffit said.

Across the street the Colbert brothers were watching with great interest.

"To ask you some questions," Clint said.

"Ask."

"Were you hired by Robert Colbert—"

"I was," Proffit said, interrupting Clint before he could finish the question, "but that hand inside changed everything." Proffit looked at Clint and asked, "Do you understand that?"

"No."

Proffit shook his head and said, "Neither do I. All I know is I can't kill you. Not after that."

"Well," Clint said, "I can't say I'm sorry to hear that, but that wasn't what I was going to ask you."

Frowning, Proffit said, "Then what was it you were going to ask me?"

"Were you hired by Robert Colbert to kill his daughter?"

Proffit stared at Clint and then started laughing.

"Is that funny?" Clint asked.

"Oh, yes," Proffit said, "it's very funny. Colbert doted on his little girl. He was all torn up when she was killed. The thought that he might have hired it done is very funny, Adams."

Clint rubbed his jaw.

"What are your ideas, then?"

"About what?"

"About who killed her."

"The man they arrested killed her."

"I don't think so."

"He was seen running from the scene."

"By a questionable witness."

"Perhaps," Proffit said, "but there was nothing questionable about the scene."

Clint frowned, berating himself again for his lack of detecting skills, or even common sense. He had never asked *where* the girl was killed.

"Why is the place she was killed so important?" he asked.

"You don't know?" Proffit asked.

"Know what?"

"Where she was killed?"

Clint gritted his teeth and said, "No, I don't know where she was killed. Are you going to tell me?"

Proffit laughed and said, "She was killed in that poor jerk's hotel room."

"What poor jerk?"

"The jerk they arrested," Proffit said. "What's his name, Tarr? The girl was killed in Justin Tarr's hotel room!"

THIRTY-FOUR

Clint felt as if he had just been punched in the stomach.

"He didn't tell you that, did he?" Proffit asked. "Tarr, I mean."

"No," Clint said, "no, he didn't tell me that."

"Seems to me you would have asked somebody about that by this time."

"I'm not a goddamned detective," Clint growled.

"Well, you're going around acting like one. I know who you are, though, Adams."

"You do?"

"Oh, yes. When Colbert hired me to . . . impede you, I did some research. I found out who you are."

Clint didn't say anything.

"The Gunsmith," Proffit said.

Clint closed his eyes. He had been hoping Proffit wouldn't say that.

"I see."

"It would have been something to see you against me," Proffit said.

"If you say so."

"I do," Proffit said. "It's too bad. You know you were followed here, don't you?"

"Yeah," Clint said, "the Colberts. At least this way I know where they are."

"Well, you go on back to your hotel. I'll keep them off your back."

Clint stared at Proffit and said, "Are you doing this just because of that hand inside?"

Proffit stared back at Clint and said, "Not *just* because of that hand."

Clint waited for the man to elaborate, then decided that he wasn't going to.

Superstition, he thought. It had very likely saved one of their lives.

As Adams walked away from the saloon Proffit crossed the street on an angle so that when he stepped up on the sidewalk he was blocking the path of Ethan and John Colbert.

"Boys," he said. "Nice night."

Ethan glared at Proffit. He didn't like the man. Proffit was everything Robert Colbert wished a son of his could be.

To Ethan, Proffit was a killer.

Well, he'd proved that he could kill, too, hadn't he?

"Get out of my way, Proffit," Ethan said.

"Am I in your way, boy?" Proffit asked.

"You better move before I have John move you," Ethan said.

"Oh, yes, your brutish brother does all your fighting for you, doesn't he, Ethan?"

"He does," Ethan said, "and I do all the thinking."

"Is that so?" Proffit said. "I rather think John here is much more suited to his task than you are to yours."

"Huh?" Ethan said, and then figured out that he'd been insulted. "John, break this fella in half."

"He works for Poppa, Ethan," John said, sounding worried.

"What does that matter?" Ethan asked. "You saw what he just did."

"What did he just do?" John asked, sounding puzzled.

"He had his chance to take care of Adams and he let him go. Now it's up to us."

"Nobody touches Adams," Proffit said, coldly. "Nobody. You tell your father I said that."

"You're crazy," Ethan said.

Proffit didn't argue that point. In fact, he almost agreed with it.

"John," Ethan said, "do it!"

Proffit knew that John, even with his wounded arm, was more than a match for him as far as strength went. He might have been able to beat the man in a fight, using his superior speed and intellect, but it would be a hell of a fight.

He wasn't in the mood.

He stepped back and produced his gun from a shoulder rig.

"Take another step, John, and I'll kill you."

"It'll take more than one bullet, Proffit," Ethan said, "and before you can fire again he'll be on you."

The hulking brute kept coming at him, and abruptly Proffit turned his gun on Ethan.

"It'll only take one shot to kill you, Ethan," Proffit said.

"John, stop!" Ethan said immediately.

"That's better," Proffit said. "Now let's us find a nice place to have a drink together."

"I don't want to drink with you!" Ethan said.

Proffit cocked the hammer on his gun and said, "I insist."

Clint returned to his hotel room in a daze and sat down on the bed.

For the first time he was having real doubts about Justin Tarr's innocence.

If Justin didn't kill the girl how had she gotten into his room to be killed there?

That was a question only Justin could answer, and come morning he was going to ask just that.

THIRTY-FIVE

"Jesus Christ," Justin Tarr said. He put his head against the bars of his cell and said in a voice filled with dread, "You think I'm guilty."

The pain in his voice was so real that Clint was already starting to have doubts about his doubts.

"I don't think you're guilty, Justin," he said, "I'm just asking how the girl got into your room."

"I don't know," Justin said. He lifted his head and looked at Clint with haunted eyes. "I walked into my room and there she was, on the bed, dead. There was blood all over."

"How did you get it on you?"

"It was on the door," he said. "It had squirted all over the room. When I walked in and saw her I backed up into the door. The inside of the door was covered with blood, and so was the doorknob. When I saw the blood on my hands I wiped them on my suit."

That was something else Clint had neglected to do. He hadn't taken a look at Justin's room. He remembered the several occasions when Allan Pinkerton—who didn't like him but respected him, and vice versa—had offered him jobs with the Pinkertons.

Would Allan still want him if he could see the way he'd handled this thing?

"All right," Clint said, "tell me why you never told me that she was killed in your room."

Justin Tarr looked at him with those big, ingenuous eyes and said, "You never asked."

"Justin," Clint said, closing his eyes, "how did she get in?"

"I don't know!" Justin said. "Come on, Clint. You've had your fair share of women. Haven't you ever gotten to your room and found a woman waiting for you?"

Clint rocked back a bit. That had happened to him more times than he could count, and any number of ruses had been used by the women involved. The latest in that line had been Alicia Colbert herself.

Had Ana Colbert gone to Justin's room on her own, or had she been taken there and killed there to implicate him in her murder?

"Justin, what was she wearing?"

"What?"

"When you found her, what was she wearing?"

"I—there was so much blood, it was hard to—to tell—I think she was—naked."

"You *think* she was naked?"

"I told you," Justin wailed, "there was so much blood."

"All right, Justin, all right, calm down," Clint said.

"Clint, you've got to believe me," Justin said, "you of all people have to believe me."

"All right, Justin, I believe you," Clint said.

Justin Tarr was no actor, he couldn't have faked the hollow eyes and the gaunt cheeks and the terror in his voice.

"I believe you," Clint said, again.

Today was Wednesday.

Justin Tarr was scheduled to hang on Friday.

Two days, Clint thought. I've got two days and what do I have?

He was shown back to the chief's office after leaving Justin.

"Well?" Chief Thoreau said.

"Well what, Chief?"

"I saw some doubt in your eyes when you came here this morning, Mr. Adams. How do you feel now?"

"The same way I've always felt, Chief," he said. "Justin Tarr is innocent."

"I feel sorry for you," the chief said.

"Why's that?"

"You'll have to watch your friend hang on Friday. Believing him innocent, that won't be very pleasant for you."

"That would be true even if I thought he was guilty, Chief," Clint said. "It's never pleasant watching a man hang."

"I wouldn't know," Thoreau said. "This will be my first."

"Take my advice, then," Clint said.

"What?"

"If we get that far," Clint said, and he fervently hoped they wouldn't, "don't eat breakfast first."

Robert Colbert was trembling with rage.

"Tell me again," he said to his son, Ethan.

"I told you already," Ethan said. "We saw Proffit and Adams together, talking like they were old buddies. When we tried to follow Adams, Proffit stopped us. He said he wanted us to bring you a message: nobody touches Adams."

"What the hell—" Colbert said. "Proffit and Adams?"

"I swear, Poppa," Ethan said.

Colbert whirled on his oldest son and slapped him in the face as hard as he could. The sound was so resounding that John, standing next to Ethan, flinched.

"What was that for?" Ethan demanded, holding his face.

"Don't ever call me that!" Robert Colbert snapped. "Why didn't you kill Adams for me?"

"I told you, Proffit held us—"

"Is all of this true, John?" Colbert said, glaring at his youngest son.

"Yes, Po—yes, sir. It's all true."

"I don't understand this," Colbert said. "Did you go into this saloon they came out of?"

"Yes, sir," Ethan said, proudly. It had been smart of them to go there after Proffit released them. "From what we heard, Adams and Proffit played poker for over three hours. On the last hand they had the bartender deal a freeze out, five cards face up, and they got exactly the same hand."

"That's impossible."

"No, sir," Ethan said. "Everybody in the place said the same thing. Except for the suits, they had exactly the same hand. The other thing is, they left the money on the table."

"What?"

"They took what they sat down with and told the bartender to give the rest to the street whores, and to tell them to take the rest of the night off."

Shaking his head Colbert said, "This gets crazier by the minute. Normally Proffit will do *anything* for money, and you're telling me that last night he was giving it away?"

"Yes . . . sir."

Colbert went around behind his desk and sat down. They were in his office, above the bank.

"Two days," he said, "in two days that murdering animal will hang. What can Adams do in two days?"

Ethan didn't know if he was supposed to answer or not, so he kept quiet.

"Two days . . ." Colbert said again, tapping his right forefinger on the desk top. Finally he looked up at his sons and said, "All right, get out!"

"Do you want us to take care of Adams?" Ethan asked.

"I want you to get out!" Colbert said. "When I want you to do something else, I'll damn well tell you. Now get the hell out!"

Ethan turned, bumped into John, glared at him and then led the way out of their father's office.

Robert Colbert sat behind the desk, worrying his bottom lip with his teeth.

What could happen in two days?

A lot, he thought, a hell of a lot.

Clint Adams was the only chance the murderer had of going free.

What was he to do now that he couldn't count on Proffit?

There was only one other person he could go to.

THIRTY-SIX

Clint went to the bank.

He decided to stop waiting for Colbert to come to him. He was going to Colbert.

As he approached the bank he saw both Ethan and John come out. Neither of them looked particularly happy, and Ethan's face was livid red on one side, as if he'd been slapped.

Clint wondered what Proffit had done to them last night.

He could have avoided them, but instead he crossed the street and his path intersected with theirs.

"You!" Ethan said.

"Me," Clint said. "You boys have a good time last night?"

"I don't know how you got Proffit over to your side, Adams, but it's not going to help you," Ethan said.

"That's good to know," Clint said. "I'll keep it in

mind. Excuse me, now, I have to see a banker."

"My father won't see you."

"Yes he will."

"Get away from here, Adams," Ethan said, "get away from New Orleans."

"Get out of my way, Ethan."

"John . . ." Ethan said, and the big man began to lumber towards Clint.

Clint reached out and gave John a good tap on his injured wrist. The big man moaned and his face went white.

"John!" Ethan said.

"Leave him alone, Ethan," Clint said. "Do your own dirty work."

"You son of a bitch!" Ethan said, and swung at Clint.

Clint easily sidestepped the punch and hit Ethan on the nose.

"Ow, damn it!" Ethan cried, his hands flying to his nose, which was bleeding.

"You'd better get that nose checked," Clint said. "It seems to bleed at the drop of a hat."

He moved around the brothers and entered the bank.

"Who?" Robert Colbert roared.

Frank Marlowe swallowed and said, "It's Clint Adams, sir—"

"I heard you the first time."

Colbert thought quickly. He opened and closed his top drawer. There was a .32 caliber revolver in there, a Colt that many people referred to as the banker's model. He wondered what kind of a chance he'd have against Adams. If he killed him behind closed doors, he could always claim that the man threatened him. That story would stand up, especially with Chief Thoreau.

"All right, Frank," he said, finally, "send him in."

"Yes, sir," Marlowe said, unable to hide his surprise.

"He'll see you," the man said to Clint. It was plain that the man was surprised.

"Thank you."

He followed the man up a flight of stairs, into a small outer office. The man approached a door and knocked, then opened it.

"Mr. Adams, sir."

Clint walked past the man into Robert Colbert's office.

He didn't know what to expect. When a man is as wealthy and powerful as a Robert Colbert you always expect to see someone who is much larger than life.

Colbert was an ordinary man. He was not tall, he was beginning to soften and his hair was thinning. For a man in his fifties he *might* have been in fairly good condition.

"Mr. Colbert," Clint said, "I think we have some things to talk about."

"Close the door, will you?" Colbert said.

Clint turned to close the door and then saw that the assistant had already closed it, silently. As he turned back he saw the gun in Colbert's hand and reacted instinctively. It was only at the last second that he did something he usually never did.

He aimed his shot away from the heart, and his bullet slammed into Robert Colbert's shoulder.

"What the hell—" he said.

"Why didn't you kill him?" Inspector Chevalier asked.

They were in Colbert's office, but Colbert had already been removed to the doctor's. Clint was now officially being questioned.

"I didn't have to," Clint said. "He was no gunman."

"No, I guess he wasn't," Chevalier said. "You know he's going to claim you threatened him."

"I expect he will. What does it mean that you already know that?"

"Not much," Chevalier said. "He's a powerful man in this state."

"So? Do I get arrested?"

"Oh, no," Chevalier said, "not right now, anyway. I'll question Colbert and then talk to the chief."

"And then?"

Chevalier grinned disarmingly and said, "Maybe *then* you'll get arrested."

THIRTY-SEVEN

They were in Chief Thoreau's office.

Clint Adams.

Inspector Chevalier.

Robert Colbert, with his arm in a sling, looking pale and unsteady.

It was the next morning. The doctor had refused to release Colbert until that morning. Clint had been asked to remain in his hotel room until the morning, and he had complied.

It was Thursday.

Justin Tarr was to hang on Friday.

"We're here to decide whether or not you should be arrested, Mr. Adams," the chief said.

"For what?"

"For trying to kill Mr. Colbert."

Clint made a face.

"If I was trying to kill Mr. Colbert he'd be dead," he said.

"Very bold talk."

"Not bold," Clint said. "Fact. You don't know my background, do you, Chief?"

"Your background? What's that got to do with it?"

Clint turned and looked at Inspector Chevalier.

"You know, don't you?"

"Yes."

"Know what?" Chief Thoreau asked.

"You want to tell him?" Chevalier asked.

"I wish you would," Clint said, and then closed his eyes and listened while the inspector told the chief who he was.

"I've heard of the Gunsmith," the chief said when the inspector finished.

"Then you know I mean what I say," Clint said. "If I'd wanted this man dead, he would be."

The chief looked at Colbert.

"Chief, if this man is not behind bars in five minutes I'll have your job."

"Wouldn't you rather know who killed your daughter, Mr. Colbert?" Clint asked. "I mean, who really killed your daughter?"

"We know who killed her," Colbert said.

"You think you know that?" Chevalier asked.

"I think I can narrow it down pretty good," Clint said.

"Go ahead," the chief said, looking at Colbert nervously.

"Chief—"

"Mr. Colbert," Chief Thoreau said, "I don't know

about you, but I'd hate to wake up Saturday morning
knowing I hung the wrong man."

"He's not—"

"For a while I thought it might be you, Inspector,"
Clint said.

"Me? Why?"

"You were avoiding me, you knew the girl, didn't
you?"

"Yes."

"Well?"

Chevalier looked at Colbert and said, "Yes."

"What does that mean?" Colbert demanded.

Clint looked at him and said, "I think it means he'd
slept with her. Is that what you meant, Inspector?"

"Yes," Chevalier said, "on several occasions."

"Impossible!" Colbert shouted. "My baby was a virgin."

"Chief," Clint said, "do you have the coroner's report there?"

"Yes."

"Would you read it to Mr. Colbert?"

The chief looked nervous.

"What's more important, Chief?" Clint asked. "Your
job, or an innocent man's life?"

Chief Thoreau took out the report and opened it.

"Which part?"

"The part pertaining to her virginity," Clint said.

The chief leaned over to read, then sat back and said,
"Oh, hell, Robert, she was no virgin."

"No," Colbert said, "she was—"

"She was pregnant, Robert," the chief said.

"What?" Colbert asked, shocked.

"Two months along," Thoreau said. "I'm sorry."

"Dan—"

Clint took a moment to wonder about the real relationship between Robert Colbert and Chief Daniel Thoreau. Could it be that they were friends and not just one man with the other in his pocket?

"But how? . . ." Colbert said.

"Well, she'd slept with the inspector, and I'm sure she'd slept with other men," Clint said, "but she'd never slept with Justin Tarr, Mr. Colbert. He didn't even know her."

"But she was found in his room."

"And you convicted him in your mind on the basis of that fact," Clint said. "Anyone could have taken her up there and killed her."

"She would have gone with anyone, too," the inspector spoke up.

"Emil—" the chief said warningly.

"No, let him talk, Chief," Colbert said. He looked at Chevalier and said, "Go ahead, Inspector."

"Forgive me, Mr. Colbert," Chevalier said, "but your daughter was . . . well, she loved men, all men, any age, size or shape. She slept with so many men there was no way she could have known who the father of the baby was."

"Dear God—" Colbert said, closing his eyes.

"She told me once . . ." Chevalier said, and then stopped.

"Told you what?" Colbert asked.

"Maybe you should ask your wife about your daughter when she was younger," the inspector said.

"How do you know all these things and I don't?" Colbert said.

"I could have loved your daughter, Mr. Colbert," Chevalier said, "if she had let me, but when I found out about the other men . . . all the other men . . . I wasn't blind . . . "

"And I was," Colbert said.

Nobody answered him.

"All of this is fine," he said, wiping a tear away with his good hand, "but it still doesn't mean he didn't kill her. She could have gone up there to sleep with him . . . "

"She didn't," Clint said.

"How do you know that?"

"I believe him when he says he didn't know her."

"There's still the witness—" the chief said, and suddenly there was a knock on the door.

"Come," the chief called out.

Officer Hautala opened the door and stepped in.

"There's a lady to see you, Chief."

"What lady?"

"Louise Killough."

Colbert stared at the officer, then his head slumped to his chest.

"Robert—" the chief said.

"Let her in, Dan."

THIRTY-EIGHT

"Are they going to prosecute Uncle Robert?" Julie asked.

"No," Clint said, "the chief convinced the state's attorney that Colbert had suffered enough."

"And what about you?"

"Colbert told the truth," Clint said.

"And you're not going to press charges against him for trying to kill you?"

"No."

"And your friend will go free?"

"As soon as the paperwork is done."

"And what about Carl Quincannon?"

"He got to take a trip to Baton Rouge."

"He'll be surprised when he comes back," she said.

"Yes, he will."

"I mean his office," she said. "It's spotless."

"He'll be shocked."

It was Friday now, and they were having lunch in the hotel.

"Why didn't the chief or the inspector tell Uncle Robert what was in the coroner's report?"

"There was a certain amount of fear involved, I guess. Your uncle *is* a powerful man, you know."

"So why'd they finally decide to go ahead and tell him what they knew?"

"He tried to kill me, and tried to have them arrest *me* for trying to kill him. It was a case that wouldn't have stood up in court."

"And yet they would have let your friend hang?"

"I hope they wouldn't have," Clint said. "I hope one of them would have said something before that happened."

"So then, who did it?" she asked.

"Killed Ana?"

"Yes."

He shrugged.

"It could have been anyone, even a man who was just passing through."

"Oh."

"It *could* have been anyone," he said again, half to himself, "but I don't think it was."

"Why not?"

"The amount of times she was stabbed," he said. "That indicates extreme anger—unless the killer was just crazy."

"Do you intend to stay around to find out who did it?"

"Not me," he said, "I'm through playing detective. I've packed my things and I'm out of here today."

"You're leaving today?" she asked, disappointed.

"Yes."

The waiter came over and asked if they wanted anything else. Clint shook his head and the man went away.

"What are you going to do?" Clint asked.

"Well, I think I'll stay a while. Aunt Alicia came to the hotel and talked to me earlier. She wants me to come to the house to have dinner tonight."

"That's a start."

"And maybe Quincannon will hire me when he sees what I did to his office."

"If the Colberts take you in you won't need a job."

"I don't want them to take me in," she said. "I just want them to acknowledge me as family."

"Well, I hope it works out."

He stood up to leave, and she remained seated.

"I'm going to go up to my room and get my gear and then check out."

"I'm going to sit here and have another cup of coffee," she said. "Maybe by the time I finish it you'll be gone."

"Good-by, Julie. Good luck."

"Good-by, Clint."

Clint retrieved his belongings from his room, checked out and headed for the livery to pick up Duke. He wondered if he should stop by the jail and see Justin, but then he had spoken to him the night before. Maybe he should have waited for Justin to get out, but he decided not to do that.

A little bit of Justin Tarr went a long way.

He entered the livery and saw that the liveryman was not there. He went to Duke's stall with the intention of saddling the big gelding himself. He threw the blanket over the horse's big back and then went to lift the saddle. He had the saddle in his hands when he realized he wasn't alone.

"Turn around," a voice said, "and hang onto the saddle."

Clint obeyed and found himself facing Ethan Colbert, who was holding a gun.

"What's this about, Ethan?"

"You," Ethan said. "You ruined it."

"Ruined what?"

"I had it planned perfectly," he said, "and now you got him off. Now they'll keep looking until they find the killer. They'll keep looking . . ."

Clint looked into the man's eyes and knew.

"You killed your sister."

"My sister," Ethan said with contempt. "She'd slept with any piece of dirt drifter who came through town, but would she sleep with me?"

"But she was your sister?"

"That didn't stop her from taking John to bed when she was thirteen. Why's he better than me?"

"Ethan—"

"For years I been after her, and for years she laughed at me. Well, I got tired of being laughed at. I decided to kill her, as soon as I found somebody to pin it on."

"And then Justin Tarr came to town."

"Yeah, Tarr," Ethan said. "I could see right off that he was a ladies' man. Everybody would believe that they were in his room together."

"How did you get her to his room?"

"She had seen him once. I knew she'd go after him sooner or later. I told her that he wanted to see her in his room, and she went up there with me."

"And you stabbed her."

"I stabbed her," Ethan said, "again and again I stabbed her—after I had her."

"You raped your sister?"

For some reason that sounded even more obscene to Clint than the fact that he'd *killed* his sister.

"Yeah, and you know what? She wasn't even that great."

"Ethan—"

"Now I'm going to kill you, because you ruined it all."

"Ethan."

This time it wasn't Clint who called his name, it was John, his brother. He'd entered the livery from behind Ethan.

"Get out of here, John."

"Ethan, let me help you—"

"Get out! Nobody can help me!"

"You need help, Ethan," Clint said, "listen to your brother."

"That moron?" Ethan said. "He didn't even know when he had it made. She would have gone to bed with him anytime, she even told me. He was so big, she said, the biggest she'd ever seen, even when he was sixteen."

"Ethan—" John said, coming up next to his brother.

"I told you to get out of here, dummy!"

"I can't, Ethan," John said. "I love you. I want to help you."

"You want to help me?" Ethan said. "Here, help me. Hold this!"

Before Clint could react Ethan turned and shot his brother. The bullet hit John in the chest and he staggered back, a look of shock on his face. He tried to stay on his feet but finally fell back onto a pile of hay.

Clint threw the saddle at Ethan, but the shock of what the man had done slowed him down. Ethan, on the other hand, moved faster than he would have thought possible and eluded the saddle.

"Hold it!" Ethan said. "Just stand still, Adams!"

"Let me help John, Ethan."

"No."

"He's your brother."

"Yeah, and I loved him, can you beat that?" Ethan said. "I loved the big dummy."

"Then why did you shoot him?"

"Because he knew, he heard us talking," Ethan said, "and now only you know."

"Wrong, Ethan."

Another new voice.

Douglas Proffit stepped out from a stall at the rear of the livery. "I know, too."

"So do I," Inspector Chevalier said. He stepped from a stall at the front of the livery.

"Wha—" Ethan said.

Neither of them had their guns out.

"Come on, Ethan," Chevalier said, "let me take you to get some help."

"What are you doing here?" Ethan shouted. "You're not supposed to be here!"

"What *are* you doing here?" Clint asked.

"I figured since you got your friend off the real killer might make a try for you before you left," Chevalier said. "With the way the girl was killed, I knew he had to be crazy—crazy enough to want to get back at you."

"And you?" Clint asked Proffit.

"I'm with him," Proffit said, inclining his head towards Chevalier. "We work together sometimes."

Clint looked from Proffit to Chevalier and saw something he hadn't seen before, but then again, he'd never seen them together.

"You're brothers," he said.

Proffit nodded.

"You knew I was looking for you because he told you," Clint said to Proffit.

"Right," Chevalier said. "We don't always get along, but sometimes we do business together."

"What kind of business?" Clint asked.

"We work both sides of the track," Chevalier said. "He makes me look real smart, sometimes."

"He's going to be chief some day," Proffit said of his brother.

"What are you talking about?" Ethan Colbert suddenly shouted. "What about me? I'm here! Don't talk to each other like I'm not here!"

"Ethan," Clint said, "put down the gun and go with the inspector. Let them get some help for John."

Proffit leaned over John Colbert and said, "I think he's going to be all right."

"He's not dead?" Ethan asked.

"No," Proffit said.

"I'm sorry, John," Ethan said, "I'm really sorry."

They all saw what was going to happen next and couldn't do anything about it.

Proffit was off balance, leaning over John.

Chevalier was too far away.

Clint was the only one who had a chance and he leaped at Ethan, shouting, "No!" but by the time he tackled him Ethan had already put the gun in his mouth and pulled the trigger.

Clint dragged a dead man down to the ground. He rolled the body over and saw that the top of Ethan's head was missing.

"Jesus," he said in disgust.

"Give me a hand," Proffit said. "We can still save this one if we get him to the doctor in time."

Clint got to his feet and went to help Proffit lift the bulky John to his feet.

"Ethan?" John said, dazed.

"Ethan's gone, John," Clint said.

"He didn't mean to shoot me," John said. "I know he didn't mean it."

"Sure, John," Clint said.

He didn't think he'd ever run across a sadder, more messed up family than the Colberts of New Orleans.

Then he thought about Chevalier and Proffit.

The lawman and the killer, working together, until the time came when they would have to face each other not as brothers, but as natural adversaries.

The lawman and the killer.

An odd pair.

Good luck.

J.R. ROBERTS
THE
GUNSMITH

Check book(s). Fill out coupon. Send to:

BERKLEY PUBLISHING GROUP
390 Murray Hill Pkwy., Dept. B
East Rutherford, NJ 07073

NAME_____

ADDRESS_____

CITY_____

STATE_____ZIP_____

**PLEASE ALLOW 6 WEEKS FOR DELIVERY.
PRICES ARE SUBJECT TO CHANGE
WITHOUT NOTICE.**

POSTAGE AND HANDLING:
$1.00 for one book, 25¢ for each additional. Do not exceed $3.50.

BOOK TOTAL $ _____

POSTAGE & HANDLING $ _____

APPLICABLE SALES TAX $ _____
(CA, NJ, NY, PA)

TOTAL AMOUNT DUE $ _____

PAYABLE IN US FUNDS.
(No cash orders accepted.)